St. Mary's H. S. Library
South Amboy, N. J.

F
Wal

Jack

FRANK WALKER

Coward, McCann & Geoghegan, Inc.

New York

Illustrations by Martin White

First American Edition 1976

Copyright © 1976 by Frank Walker

All rights reserved. This book, or parts thereof, may not be reproduced in any form without permission in writing from the publisher.

SBN: 698-10752-7

Library of Congress Cataloging in Publication Data

Walker, Frank, 1930-
    Jack.

    I. Title.
PZ4.W17814Jac3   [PR6073.A4115]   823'.9'14   76-13471

Printed in the United States of America

I would like to thank the Leeds branch of the Associated Sheep, Police, and Army Dog Society, for teaching me what little I know about dog handling and how to care for and enjoy a dog.

Frank Walker

Jack

Chapter 1

(I)

The first thing Jack ever saw was a broad, brilliant shaft of April sunlight coming in over the open top half of the kennel door. The sudden incomprehensible way his eyes started to work frightened him and he blundered, or rather, staggered through his crawling brothers and sisters to the warmth of his mother's belly and the comfort of a teat. He sucked greedily, closing his eyes against the offending brightness and when his stomach was full he slept, oblivious of other small bodies trying to nudge him out of the way to get at the milk.

He wasn't called Jack then, he wasn't called anything, he was just one of a litter of three dogs and four bitches, fumbling his way about the airy, dry kennel, growing stronger and sniffing in his first breaths of life, exploring sightlessly and bravely up to distances which were all of three feet from his mother's breasts. Any alien sound sent him back to her protection as fast as his unsteady legs could force a way through or over the other tiny, yielding bodies.

Until his vision came, his had been a safe, warm world with nothing to do but feed and sleep and try out his legs and learn the difference between the smell of his mother and that of the something which came into the kennel every day with a clanking bucket to make strange noises. At first, the strange presence had bewildered Jack but eventually he'd got used to it and had learned to know what the squeak of the bolt meant. Once, to his terror, he had been taken up from the ground and pressed close to something smooth and the soothing noises in his ear had done nothing to lessen his fear. He'd worked his legs weakly and twisted his body until he'd been placed back on the safe ground.

He didn't know it, but he was the son of champions, Belgian Sheepdogs, a hardy breed whose ancestors had been particularly developed as much for fighting the wolves as for herding the sheep of the European plains. Combined in his make-up were the careful gentleness of a true working animal with the ferocious tenacity of natural guard and protector. His baby coat, jet black and softly fuzzy, would give way to a long and thick luxurious growth just as black as his present fluff except for a white 'cravat' on his throat and chest. He would be equipped with double insulation which would keep out cold or heat and his body heat in, making him a dog which could live comfortably in rigorous temperatures at either end of the thermometer. He would come into the category of Large Dog, he would be twenty-four to twenty-six inches high at the withers and about the same distance from chest to rump but his most desirable quality would be his adaptability to training—if he ran true to the breed—for exceptional parents do not necessarily produce like offspring.

Hunger woke him again and when he opened his eyes for the second time, it was dark in the kennel but over the open top half of the door he could see the clear night sky with glittering stars and the pale light of the hidden moon. He liked this better, this didn't frighten him and he walked across to examine the bar of lightness coming underneath the lower door. When he'd looked at it long enough he went back to fill his stomach from his patient mother and sleep again. The hoot of an owl disturbed him in the early hours and he lay watching his first dawn. Because the light came steadily he was not afraid any more and in the course of that day he found out the wild excitement of visual exploration.

The first thing to interest him was his mother. Lying on her side and watching his progress with soft brown eyes, she looked massive to Jack with the six other pups more or less confining themselves to the area marked by her stretched fore and hind-legs. When he went to examine the expressive face with the intelligent eyes, a red tongue came out to lick him. He liked being licked and lay down as his mother washed him. She started with his face and went on over his head, down his back and sides, and he made sounds that would have been more appropriate coming from a kitten.

At this stage of his life nothing would hold his attention for long and before his bath was complete, he saw the feeding dishes against the wall and went to see what they were. His mother watched him cross the wooden floor, then turned to look over her shoulder to see how the rest of the litter were faring. Very shortly they would all be able to see and the kennel would be transformed from a quiet maternity room into a boisterous kindergarten.

Jack looked over the edge of the feeding dishes and although the one for the meat had a strange exciting smell it was empty but the second one held something which reflected the light into his eyes. He didn't like that and scuttled back to his mother. It wasn't long before his courage returned and he set out to see the darker corners of the kennel but apart from his mother, the rest of the family and the feeding dishes, there was nothing to occupy the mind of an inquisitive youngster. Then a big thing happened.

He was prodding his way through the litter to get at

the milk when the light was partly blotted out and the squeak of the bolt told him the carrier of the thing that clanked was coming. He looked round and looked up, and up, and up at the huge thing standing in the doorway. He knew by the smell that it was the bucket carrier but this time there was no bucket. But Jack wasn't frightened. The eyes looking down at him were warm and friendly like his mother's and although he'd never seen a smile the expression on the round, red face gave him confidence. Even when he was picked up in a big, roughened but gentle hand, turned this way and that as he was looked at expertly, he didn't struggle to get down. In fact he liked it; it gave him the same sense of security as when his mother licked him.

'Jane!'

The booming noise startled Jack at first but after the initial shock when he found he hadn't been hurt, he lay still again and was turned on to his back. Two fingers tickled his belly. Jack squirmed ecstatically.

'What's the matter?'

Another of the big creatures was there now and Jack was passed to a smaller pair of hands and held close to a smooth cheek. He heard again the soothing murmurings which had disturbed him when he'd still been blind. 'What a lovely boy. He's just like a bear cub, Wilf. He's going to be big, though.'

Wilf snorted. 'You're at it again, how many more times have I to tell you, you can't tell a thing about 'em at that age. If you could, we'd be left with all them that wasn't going to grow up good enough for the show ring, wouldn't we?'

Jane held Jack on her left forearm, stroking him with her right hand.

'You are going to be a big boy, aren't you?' she cooed. Wilf snorted again and marched away from the whelping kennels, leaving his wife to utter her idiocies to herself. She put Jack down, picked up the other pups in turn and when she was satisfied they were all well she opened the door. 'Come on, Bess, time you had a walk.'

Jack's mother got to her feet to follow Jane out into the yard and as he tried to follow, the door closed and Jane leaned over. 'Not yet, little feller, when you're a bit bigger.'

Jack wanted to go with his mother. He stood at the bottom of the door whimpering and trying to look under the narrow gap but it was no good, she'd gone and he couldn't get out. Something moved beside him and he looked up into the eyes of one of his sisters. He saw intelligence there and forgot his mother in the newly discovered companionship. They looked at each other, then sniffed, pushed and went together to see what the still blind ones were doing. His mother came back after a little while to have her belly attacked by seven hungry mouths. Jack, with his advantage of sight, was first to a teat, first to gorge, roll over and go to sleep. His initial hours of awareness had tired him out.

Every day of the weeks that followed held something new and wonderful. When the litter had built up sufficient energy and self-assuredness in moving about they were let out into the large yard with Bess for a daily romp. Jack loved this, the hurly burly of mock fights, all the holes and corners to be looked into and evaluated as points of interest. And as much as this he liked the weaning process, the gradual introduction of semi-solid foods four times a day to break him from dependancy on his mother.

As he neared the eighth week of his life more and more strange people came to see him, pick him up and stroke him and he loved every minute of it. Had he known he was witnessing discussions of his possible sale which would result in a permanent parting with his mother, his reception of the strangers would have been very different. But he didn't know that so he would run to the door to greet the newcomers every time it was opened.

On Jack's sixtieth day of life, Wilf and Jane came into the yard where the pups were frolicking around Bess and with them was a stranger who, when Jack was picked up, wasn't a total stranger. Jack recognised the smell and voice from the previous week.

'I've made my mind up, Wilf, I'll take this feller.'

Jack basked under the spell of the stranger's belly-tickling.

Wilf shrugged. 'Just as you like, Tom, but it looks as though the missus was right. He's growing like a bloody beanstalk ... looks as though he'll be too big for showing.'

Tom tucked Jack under his arm and Jack sniffed at his sheepskin coat, not flustered. He'd be put down again soon to go back to Bess.

'I told you I've finished with showing,' Tom grunted. 'It's a good workin' dog I want for the estate, ready for when old Rex is finished. He can't go on for ever. He's nearly twelve now, you know.'

'All right,' Wilf said, 'it's your money. Fetch him in the house and I'll get you his pedigree.'

The wonderland indoors held Jack's attention and he'd no time to think about his mother. There was a forest of chair and table legs, a low sofa to get wedged under and a rug to roll on when he had explored everywhere else. Tom was watching his antics as he spoke to Wilf.

'Full o' beans, isn't he? Think I'll call him Jack.'

Wilf was signing Jack's life over to Tom's care and he looked up. 'Good and simple, but he'll have to have a kennel name just in case. Bess's show name's Isabella De Montpelier, so how about Jacques De Montpelier?'

Tom leaned forward to click his fingers in front of Jack's nose.

'Come here, Jacques De Montpelier.' He chuckled, 'Aye, put that down, but it'll never get used.' He drummed his fingers on the floor and when Jack went to investigate he scooped him up to his knee. 'Now listen to me Jack, you're going to be spoiled to hell for the next couple o' months with my kids but after that you'll start your training, d'you hear, and you'll be the best workin' dog in the country when old Rex has gone—you'd better be, I'm payin' a bloody fortune for you.'

Wilf passed over the envelope containing Jack's family tree and a receipt for forty-five pounds.

'You could put him in an obedience show or two, and if he's any good you'll get your money back in stud fees.'

Tom paused in the doorway. 'I might do that if he shows any promise.' He laughed again and put Jack back under his arm. 'Don't suppose you'd mind the odd bitch now and then in a year or two, eh Jack? See you later then, Wilf, say cheerio to Jane for me.'

He spoke soothingly all the way out of the front of the house to where his Land Rover was parked and the vista that opened up with the front door served to keep Jack from fretting for Bess a while longer.

There was so *much* to look at this first time Jack saw the world outside the kennel yard, he didn't know *what* to look at first. There were trees and a flower garden and his quick eyes picked out the flying insects flitting about the blooms. Whenever he looked up there were birds in the sky idly wheeling or flashing quickly in the spring sunshine and off to the left, behind a hedge, bitches and dogs barked at each other from their separate compounds. Jack knew what a bark was, he'd heard Bess venting her joy when they'd been let out into the yard and vaguely he realised that there were others like her in the world.

At the bottom of the garden they went through a wicket gate to the road and Jack cringed into Tom's chest when a sports car thundered by. Tom stroked his head.

'Oh you'll like cars all right when you get to know what they're for.'

From his own Land Rover parked at the kerb came another bark, a bark of welcome when Rex, a long-haired Alsatian, saw them coming. Tom opened the door, holding Jack out to be sniffed at and accepted. 'How about this feller, Rex? Will he do for an understudy? Get over, then.'

The old dog went over on to the rear seat and Tom carefully put Jack on the front passenger seat. 'Now then, let's get home and see what the family think of you.'

Rex hadn't completed his examination of the new boy and hung his great head over the back of the seat to have a more selective and protracted sniff. When the engine burst into life, Rex took no notice but Jack sat bolt upright, trembling at the strange sound and when the car moved off he began to whimper and miss Bess.

Tom never stopped talking on that journey. He knew the puzzled fear of the total strangeness of all the things his pup would be feeling, he knew that from time to time the fretful pangs for his missing mother would make him mew and cry but he also knew the only way to transfer the infant affection from Bess to himself was by unstinting, unfailing kindness. Jack couldn't understand a word he said but like all of his kind he could tell the difference in tones of voice and the low, happy words at least stilled his fears of travelling.

It was a long drive from the low-lying agricultural plain with its scattered trees up into the high country of rolling hills, noisy streams, stretching moors and isolated copses; game country where pheasant, partridge, duck, roe-deer, grouse, salmon and trout battled with puny muscles but developed wits against hawk, eagle, fox, otter, stoat and weasel. A throwback piece of country to the days when poachers carried longbows and goose-fletched arrows and a hangman's noose was the price of failure instead of a fine awarded with a hidden chuckle.

A far-sighted ancestor had seen the pillage to come to the open country with the birth of the Industrial Revolution and had set up a permanent trust, with money squeezed from hellish weaving sheds, to ensure the perpetual continuance of Scargill estate so that those who could afford to pay for the privilege, could come and hunt. Tom Ewing was the Estate Manager and to him a trained dog was as important as his right arm—a swift, far-reaching, dependable right arm. So he talked himself dry to put the pup at ease and forge the first thread of affection.

On the back seat the old dog, a seasoned traveller, slept. In the front passenger seat the infant dog gazed at the tops of the flashing scenery as the vehicle sped steadily upward. The last of the green hedgerows passed and the first of the dry stone walls, craggy, bleak and solid, appeared. The vegetation changed too, from deep green, lush pasture and young corn to the paler green of hill grass with its patches of heather and gorse. Here and there a boulder protruded through the grass and many a hillcrest was capped with stark, black granite. Jack was going home to a wild and free country where a grown dog was feared by predator and vermin, human or otherwise.

If his future charges and enemies could have seen him then, small and perplexed, they wouldn't have feared him, especially when Tom Ewing had twice to stop the Land Rover to lift Jack and mop up small puddles. Tom didn't scold him for his indiscretions, he merely said the word, 'No', repeatedly in a stern, unfriendly tone. Jack would come to understand what 'No' meant later and Tom was merely introducing him to the voice changes which would have the greatest influence on him when they started training in earnest. But that time was weeks away, the first business was to let Jack see he was one of the family, that people would care for and feed him, and to make sure Jack knew where he lived. In return Jack would have to give obedience and loyalty at all times and in any conditions.

Eventually his weariness overcame his excitement and he slept for the last few miles. It was the bumpy progress over the private track which led into the heart of the estate that awakened him. Rex woke too and hung his questing head down again for another sniff at Jack. Jack sniffed back and a big tongue licked his head. He lay on his side for more but Rex was satisfied and disappeared into the rear. Jack remembered Bess and whined.

Tom's home was called Scargill Croft although it would be hard to imagine anything less croft-like. It was the original home of the first owner of the estate, a spacious two storey house of grey Yorkshire stone with an everlasting thatched roof. Built in a pleasant green bowl formed by a ring of hills, the brunt of the winter winds whistled harmlessly far above it and in summer the depression caught and held the heat of the sun. But because it was in high country the air was never humid or heavy but as clear and sweet as an unpolluted atmosphere can be, invigorating, health promoting and appetite building. The house was surrounded by an unfenced garden at the front and sides, whilst to the rear chickens and ducks ranged in the safety of spacious pens. The wire netting kept away the foxes and larger killers and two neutered she-cats left sufficient scent lying about to discourage rats.

Jack saw three people come round the side of the house to meet the Land Rover, Agnes, Tom's large smiling wife and his children, Philip, a robust ten-year-old and Marjorie who was nine. The children were at the side of the vehicle looking in before Tom had time to set the handbrake and Marjorie yelled, 'He's brought him, Mam, he's lovely. Can I hold him, Dad? We're goin' to call him Simon.'

'Whoa!' Tom opened the door and passed Jack out into eager hands. '*You're* not calling him anything, he's already got a name. How about Jacques De Montpelier?'

Philip grimaced. '*That's* not a name for a dog. Everybody'll laugh at him.'

Tom got out and stretched thankfully. 'Try Jack, then, and that's his name so don't let me hear you two calling him anything else.'

Agnes laughed as she took her turn at holding the new arrival, 'As if they'd dream of such a thing.'

Tom grunted. 'Not much they wouldn't! But they've been warned.'

Jack was all eyes, ears and nose as he took in the strange surroundings and showed a special interest in the clucking and quacking birds as they entered the house by the kitchen door at the rear. And his inquisitiveness was sharpened by the delicious smells coming from the oven and pans on the cooker. Rex trailed in nonchalantly last, showing his disdain with a huge yawn as he lay down in his corner. Tom took Jack from Philip and put him on the floor. 'Go on then, you'd better have a look round and get used to the place.'

Jack didn't need telling. He was under the table, under the dresser, under the sink, round chair legs and finished up abruptly, with his nose two inches from Rex's. The old dog stared back, unmoved. Jack made three stiff-legged hops backward, then ran back and forth the length of Rex's reclining body. Rex yawned again, licked his lips and closed his eyes, flatly refusing the indignity of romping about with a mere stripling, for Rex was over eighty years old by human standards and had used all his diminishing energy on the daily tour of the estate.

Jack cocked his head in one last try and was answered by a soft, canine snore. He gave it up and turned to attack the piece of rag Philip was wiggling on the ground but he stopped suddenly in mid-charge, head back, ears up, staring at the open door. Two unwinking green eyes gazed back haughtily, full of contempt.

'It's only Matilda,' Marjorie informed Jack as though that explained everything. It explained nothing to Jack. Deep in his being a tiny unease stirred, a vague restlessness that was the beginning of the hatred of all things feline that was bred into him. Had the meeting occurred a few months later, when his instincts were more mature, he wouldn't have hesitated in trying to put an end to Matilda's life but at that moment he was very young and unsure. Tom picked him up and walked slowly across the room to the immobile tortoiseshell. He squatted down, stroking Jack, talking all the time, 'There y' are, y' see, it's only old Mattie the rat catcher.' He ran a hand along the silky back and stiffening tail, gently putting Jack down close to her. For seconds the cold green eyes stared into the pup's brown ones, then Matilda stalked arrogantly across to her milk saucer in the corner opposite Rex's. It was empty but a plaintive mew soon had a milk bottle gurgling into it. Jack realised he was thirsty and before Tom could stop him he'd run to push his head down beside the cat's and show off his newly acquired lapping technique. Matilda didn't seem to mind, in fact she didn't even condescend to acknowledge the presence of the greedy intruder.

'Well,' Agnes said as she watched, 'if Matilda's accepted him, he's nothing to fear from Spooky. Come on, Marje, help me lay the table, dinner's just about ready.'

To Jack, this new place he found himself in was a wonderland of surprises with something new and exciting happening every second. He dashed here, there, and everywhere, hardly digesting the sight of Agnes straining cabbage before he was running over to watch Marjorie buttering bread. Then there was Tom lifting the roast beef from the oven and a trip back to the table to see him carve. When Tom took the sizzling tray of roast potatoes from the oven the smells and all the unaccustomed company were too much for Jack. He gave vent to his excitement by wetting the stone floor. Marjorie, who could hardly take her eyes off him, shrieked with delight, 'Mam, Dad, he's christened the floor.'

Tom put the carver down and said heavily, 'Oh, has he. He christened the seats in the Land Rover twice on the way home. Come here, Jack.'

Jack was skittering away for another drink of Matilda's milk but Tom caught him and took him back to the puddle.

'No,' he said severely, 'no, no!'

He carried him to the door where Philip was spreading a newspaper in preparation for Jack's first piece of instruction. He sat him in the centre of page three and tickled his throat.

'That's a good boy, Jack, you come and make your messes on this paper till you're old enough to go outside on your own.'

That was all, and Jack was free to roam the kitchen again. Whilst Agnes was serving the meal Tom made Jack's first dinner. Beaten egg with crumbled brown bread and a dish of milk. Jack wasn't slow at anything, least of all eating and the family had hardly sat around the table before he was threading his way in and out of their chairs, full of curiosity over what was going on out of his sight. Tom looked down and pointed his fork. 'You'll get nothing off this table, lad, so you might as well go and lie down with Rex. He'll show you the ropes.'

Jack stood looking up hopefully and when Tom ignored him he tried Agnes, then Philip, then Marjorie. Marjorie knew the rules perfectly well; that no animal should be fed from the table and that her father insisted on any animal living in that household being properly trained which included *not* begging for food at the table. But Jack was a novelty, the first pup she had known, Rex being older than she, and he looked so small and appealing to the girl that she looked at her father from under her brows.

'Da-ad.'

Tom didn't take his eyes from the plate. He'd been waiting for it and growled, 'No, and don't ask again. Give that dog any bad habits now and I'll have a hell of a job breaking him of them later—not to mention the fact that he might choke on that lump of meat you've pushed to the side of your plate.'

Marjorie sighed. Philip laughed.

'Idiot, you ought to have more sense than ...'

'Don't call me an idiot, Big Ears, I'll ...'

'That's enough!' Agnes snapped, and Jack wandered around listening to the click of knives and forks until the meal was over. The seal had been set on what would be Jack's future behaviour pattern.

Healthy young boys, like healthy pups, don't take long over a meal and Philip was the first to finish. He pushed his chair back. 'Can I take Jack out in the garden, Dad?'

'Aye, show him around and start making him understand that chickens and ducks are for human consumption. He'll soon get the idea.'

If the inside of the house had been an Aladdin's Cave to Jack, the big open garden was a paradise. He ran everywhere, chased by the yelling children who were shouting a stream of contradictory orders of which he didn't understand a word. Through the beds of tender, young lettuce and in and out of the pea canes, across the potato patch and then a brief halt to look at what remained of the strawberry crop. He couldn't resist a foray into the maze of currant bushes and right in the centre he met the final member of his family, Spooky, the other she-cat, jet black in colour and larger than Matilda. Jack stood rigid in the soft soil as Spooky came silently, sinuously to look at the stranger. She stared for a long moment and then unexpectedly streaked away after a sparrow who'd had the temerity to land and look for food on the path between the two pens. Jack followed curiously and was immediately roused by the strange noises made by the waddling, white birds, most of which were followed by a platoon of ducklings. The yellow, puff-ball chicks in the other pen, however, had no such order of movement and darted willy-nilly like so many clockwork mice all around their mother's legs. It was a very extraordinary and incomprehensible world, but very stimulating and he dodged Philip's hands to dash back towards the house.

They gave him an hour or so to start finding his way about and then Tom took him in to show him his bed. It was a low-sided cardboard box with a piece of rug on the bottom covered with sheets of newspaper. After a brief but inevitable inspection of the box, Jack flopped on his side and was asleep almost before his head touched the paper.

Tom grinned. 'He's due for another feed at about eight, reckon we'll have to wake him up for it—and remember,' he turned to his children, 'no matter how much he cries tonight, you two stop in bed. No comin' out here to pet him.'

Jack was duly tickled into wakefulness at eight o'clock when Rex was given his one meal of the day. They ate side by side from plastic bowls big enough to hold two pounds of meat which was the daily ration of a full-grown large dog and Jack's little heap of minced meat and cereals looked minute compared with the old dog's pile of red chunks, but it would be necessary for Jack to eat four small amounts each day for another two or three months.

He was, of course, first to finish and turned his inquisitive nose to see what Rex was enjoying so much. Rex didn't even bother to look up. A low rumbling growl of warning came from the huge throat. Jack didn't know a warning when he heard one and was rash enough to put his head over the rim of his senior's bowl. Rex swung his head sideways, rolling Jack over in a furry ball and immediately swung it back to continue his meal. Jack thought it was a game and dashed back into the fun. This time Rex turned his grey muzzle and the black lips drew back over the yellow teeth and he gave Jack the benefit of the fearsome snarl he normally saved for intruders, human or otherwise, on the estate. Even for one so young there was no mistaking what that meant and he went across to have a look at the milk situation in the cat's saucer. He had been watched by four pairs of amused eyes, the Ewings knowing there was no danger of Rex attacking him, and Tom said, 'Now there's a little feller who's quick on the uptake. Maybe I'll be able to make something of him. Jack!'

Jack took no notice until he heard milk being poured into his own drinking bowl and then he lost interest in the cat's rations.

That evening the Ewing children—unbelievably in their mother's eyes—ignored the television in the sitting room to play with Jack in the kitchen. Jack had tried to follow Tom through the hall when he went to teleview and he was quickly put back in his place on the stone floor and again he heard the stern, '*No*', repeated several times. And in the midst of play, when he started to squat down to relieve himself he was snatched up, rushed across the room and deposited on the newspapers. There he obligingly did his duty and was told what a good boy he was and when it came to bedtime for the children, the first tiny seeds of what would be built up into a true, unbending discipline, had been sown in his infant mind.

Much later, when it was dark, when Rex slept and the cats were out on their nocturnal patrols, Jack woke up and automatically nuzzled about for his mother's teat but all he touched were the sides of his box. After a frantic scramble, he escaped from the confines of his bed and moved about the hard floor searching for her, not being able to grasp why she wasn't there to comfort him when she had always been there before when it was dark. He got himself lost in the pitch blackness but by accident he stumbled on Rex and curled up with his puppy-down tight against the dense, long coat of the Alsatian. He knew this wasn't his mother but Rex's body rose and fell with breathing just like Bess's and the steady movement with the soft, sighing breaths lulled Jack back into a peaceful sleep which held him for the rest of the night.

The sound of the door to the hall opening and Tom's voice, finally woke him.

'Come an' look at this, Agnes, it looks as though Rex has been adopted for a father.'

Agnes laughed. 'Yes, poor little chap, he'll be missing his mother although I didn't hear him crying once.'

Nor had Tom. 'He maybe felt safe enough having Rex to cuddle up to. Good job anyway, he'll forget her all the quicker with a bit of company.'

The fears of the night left Jack when Agnes started to cook breakfast and the aroma of frying bacon filled the kitchen. It was as though he'd never seen the kitchen before and nothing would do until he had closely inspected everything again, every piece of furniture and every corner.

He'd wet the floor only once on his midnight prowl but he was shown the damp patch, told, '*No*' and placed on the newspapers with much stroking and patting.

Unlike Rex he got a breakfast, the same cereals as Philip and Marjorie but well pulped up in milk and after the meal he was taken out into the yard again to orientate himself with the local geography. He came out of the currant bushes in time to see Tom and Rex leaving in the Land Rover on the daily round of poacher detecting. In a few months, when he'd learned the rudiments of obedience, his life's work would start and he'd go with them but until then he had the freedom of the kitchen and garden, the children to play with when they weren't at school and his four meals a day to keep him occupied. A very full life for a lively pup not yet nine weeks old and Jack piled in with gusto, ready for any kind of game at any time—except when his energy temporarily ran out, then he slept wherever he happened to be, to recuperate.

Chapter 2

(2)

After a month it is doubtful whether Jack ever thought about Bess and after two months it was quite likely he wouldn't have known her if she'd come into the kitchen of Scargill Croft. The young of all species have short memories and puppy dogs no less than the others. In point of fact, it's not impossible that he looked on Agnes as his mother in his early days. It was she who kept his drinking dish filled with water and gave him his two middle-of-the-day meals when Tom was out and the children at school. It was she who gently scolded him and washed the mud from his body in wet weather and it was to her he went for comfort in the decreasing periods of loneliness of those first two months and she never sent him away. Whatever household task she was in the middle of, she never failed to break off to bend down to stroke and pet him for a few moments and then find some plaything to keep his mind occupied. But never was he picked up and cuddled nor allowed to jump up and put his paws on anyone. Tom had told the children sternly that this dog wasn't going to be allowed to develop even one bad habit and he'd better not catch either of them with Jack on their knees. Not that Jack didn't try to melt their hearts with his soft brown eyes and yaps of pleasure whenever anyone returned home and in the early weeks he'd wet the floor three times with excitement when Tom walked through the door.

Gradually, though, he became housetrained, learning first what the newspapers by the door were for and then still using them when they'd been transferred out into the back garden. When he regularly went to the door to be let out, the newspaper routine was abolished and he'd absorbed his first and most important lesson. Agnes also taught him his first three words of command by breaking off her work at odd moments to make him sit, lie down and stay. This was as far as she took his education and Tom would carry on the obedience training when Jack was about half grown.

These summer days of puppyhood were glorious for Jack. In his mind the whelping kennels might never have existed and it was as though the wild free land around Scargill Croft was the only location he'd ever known—which when all was boiled down, was just about the truth. As his body grew, so did his curiosity and his world of the gardens and fowl-runs became too small for his active mind.

His first trip into the outside consisted of a lolloping run round the perimeter of the cultivated land and he was back ferreting about near the greenhouse before Agnes knew he'd been away. He hadn't strayed far, a mere few yards outside the territory he knew, but it had been an adventure for him and he had enjoyed his first taste of roaming. The following day when the children had gone on the school bus and Rex had gone with Tom in the Land Rover, he trotted again round the top end of the currant bushes and on to the stubbly, springy moorland turf. The heat of the sun was counteracted by a brisk, westerly breeze which ruffled Jack's growing coat and carried all kinds of new, wonderful scents to his improving sense of smell; scents which were blanketed in the garden by those of the vegetables and birds.

The circuit he started on was wider than that of the previous day and his gait responded to the thrill of freedom. He moved quickly, passed the end of the bushes, the celery beds, the potato patch and round the corner of the duck pen. He stopped there to scratch his shoulder with a hind paw and picked up his first rabbit trail. His original intention of going round the garden to the house was forgotten and he set off at speed with his nose close to the ground on the ruler-straight rabbit run. He was halfway up the hill at the rear of the house, one of the hills which formed the bowl, when Agnes saw him through the kitchen window where she was washing the breakfast dishes. Soapy water dripping from her hands she ran to the door and shouted, almost screamed, 'Jack! Jack!'

Jack didn't even pause and she watched helplessly as he breasted the rise and vanished over the far side.

He'd heard her all right but at that moment Agnes was of no consequence at all. Under his nostrils was the warm smell of something which he instinctively knew couldn't be too far in front of him. He gave no thought to what would happen if or when he ran his quarry down, that didn't matter. What mattered was the chase, the exhilarating joy of trailing something that was alive, and judging by the smell, edible. He ran with all the concentration of a cheetah after a gazelle but with his nose to guide him instead of his eyes. Had his throat been fully mature he would have been barking for the sheer joy of living.

Over the first hill, the country out of the bowl rolled in shortening waves until it was broken and boulder strewn and cut with rivulets and streams. Here the rabbit had perforce to change direction many times and Jack snuffled happily on into one cluster of rocks where the scent ended. It ended at a hole in the ground but inside the hole and on the earth all about it the scent was stronger with slight variations where many rabbits had played in the moonlight.

But from Jack's point of view it wasn't a wasted journey. The rocks themselves in their untidy scattering, threaded everywhere with rabbit scent, warranted a full investigation and he sniffed around busily, finding two more entrances to the burrow. He was in his element here, darting about, poking into all the nooks and crannies, and at the far side of the rocks from where he'd entered he picked up another, completely different smell. A strong pungent trail, a little fresher than that of the rabbit's and very easy to follow. He didn't hesitate and bounded off in the acrid wake of another mysterious something on a course which led him farther away from home. It seemed the world was full of riddles to solve.

His spirits were as high as only an innocent pup's can be with a mind still free from thoughts of danger, hunger or thirst. His only concern was to find out what kind of creature had left this unmistakable trail. For half an hour it led due south, then south-east and finally at an acute angle to the west. On the western leg he came across his first tragedy and the trail took him straight to it.

There was an area of scattered destruction in a small hollow and the smell of blood was strong. Here and there were brown feathers amongst a clutch of empty, broken eggshells, a quiet, sad scene which told the age old story of the survival of the strongest, providing the finder knew the ways of nature. Jack didn't. He stopped briefly to lick at the albumen sticking to the insides of the shells and picked up the trail again. It led now, apart from bending round high rocks, as straight as a rabbit run and still to the west. It was also much fresher because of the halt to kill the partridge and eat the eggs, so strong Jack could follow it with his head up in the normal position and faintly on the air he detected the scent of the dead partridge.

He was heading directly at a thick copse of trees growing on top of a rounded hill and knew instinctively that it was in those trees the trail would end. He quickened his pace to get to the end of the journey for he was tiring fast now and wanted to see the quarry before he slept. He still hadn't reached the foot of the hill when it happened. His left foreleg was snatched in a hard, painful grip, tripping him so he turned over in the air and fell sideways on the springy turf. The fall didn't hurt him but the thing biting on his leg made him yelp. His first reaction was fright and fear of the thing holding him and he struggled to pull away from it. The more he pulled the harder it bit him and his cries were continuous as he fought to escape. Eventually he stopped from sheer exhaustion and lay down to regain his breath and look at his attacker. It was what he would come to know as a rabbit snare, a loop of strong wire camouflaged with a covering of green plastic and fastened securely to a long wooden peg driven deeply into the ground. He couldn't see the noose because it was pulled so tight with his struggle that it was buried in the skin under his hair. As he watched, a drop of blood oozed out. He licked at the blood and whimpered quietly.

The sun was high and warm on his back, the grass soft and comforting under his belly and his fatigue overcame him, deadening the pain and the urge to drink. He lowered his head to the ground and slept. To his left a buck rabbit, who had come to the mouth of the bolt hole to see what was causing the disturbance, blinked and went back to his bed. From high overhead an old hawk considered the possibility of eating him but he could see Jack was breathing and even though he was not yet half-grown the hawk decided not to take any chances. Very few animals of prey will tackle a creature which may successfully fight back, including hawks, and that hawk didn't know Jack was so young and helpless and handicapped.

The sun was well over the zenith when Jack woke and for a moment he was fuddled, not remembering where he was and how he got there. When he tried to rise, the snare bit him again, and again he panicked, pulling backward and dragging the wire deeper into his flesh, disturbing the congealed blood and starting a new, stronger flow. He lay down again, defeated, to lick the blood away and try to ease the pain.

He had no conception of time and as the hours passed he was only aware of the hurt and a worsening thirst. What thoughts he had were of Tom and Agnes, knowing he desperately wanted them to come and release him, take him home to feed him and give him a drink. From time to time he would whimper and lick at the encrusted blood and look hopefully in the direction of home. Presently he slept again, the deep heavy sleep of the sick.

It was the cold which woke him the second time. If he'd had his full, adult coat he could have slept outdoors without harm in the middle of winter but his hair was still short and lacking in insulation. Also he had a slight fever which made him shiver violently. It was night time although he could see clearly enough in the moonlight. He could see rabbits watching him suspiciously from where they sat in close proximity to the burrow ready to dart inside if he turned out to be dangerous. When he lay still they became bolder and hopped a few yards towards him and Jack whimpered at them, not knowing what they were but grateful to have something alive, close to him. It was comforting he wanted and to be taken home so he appealed to the rabbits in vain, but after freezing at his first sound, they carried on with their feeding and playing and stayed where he could see them; the company of rabbits was better than no company at all.

Jack didn't actually sleep again, the throbbing pain in his leg wouldn't let him, but he dozed regularly in catnaps, his head drooping down to his paws and snapping up again when he woke. He gained awareness for the umpteenth time very late in the night when the moon was high, to find the rabbits had gone and when he looked around for them he saw why. His agony momentarily forgotten he sprang to his feet to face what his instinct told him was danger. The sharp smell he'd been trailing when he'd run into the snare was emanating strongly from an animal sitting twenty yards away watching him. This animal sat upright like a dog and was like a dog in many respects with a pointed face, pointed ears and very sharp looking pointed teeth. It had a bushy coat and tail which looked dark brown in the pale moonlight and its hungry eyes never left Jack. A few small eggs and one partridge was a poor night's feeding for a pair of foxes with twin cubs.

As if materialising from the ground the vixen came to sit two yards to the dog's right and her belly was as empty as her mate's but here before them, helpless and ready for the taking was a cub of one of the dogs that men used to hound and kill foxes. And dog fashion, she licked her lips.

In absolute silence and as though it had been rehearsed many times the foxes moved apart, running in a semicircle until Jack was directly between them. There they sat again, in no hurry, testing and checking that this wasn't a trap and there was no danger to themselves, for it is by ultra caution that foxes manage to live as long as they do in an entirely hostile world where every living thing is their enemy. A too sudden charge can end easily in death and this pair was experienced in the art of survival, unwilling to take even the smallest risk.

Jack's young hackles rose as he faced the dog and then the vixen, knowing that no good could come to him of this encounter but having no conception that they were going to tear him to pieces and eat him. Even if he hadn't been hampered by a badly damaged leg his juvenile strength and small teeth would have been no match for either of the foxes and he had to face them both.

His movements had started the blood trickling from his leg again and there is nothing that excites a hungry fox more than the smell of fresh blood. Satisfied there was no peril, the dog fox licked his slavering lips and started to move forward cautiously on his short legs and Jack could see the moon reflecting clearly from the merciless eyes. At the same time the vixen began to close in and the distance between all three animals, from fox to fox, was no more than five yards. Here they stopped again to test the air with twitching ears and sensitive nostrils as at this range the man smell on Jack, rubbed there by much contact with Tom and Agnes, reached them and above all things on earth they feared man the most. It puzzled them that this pup should carry two scents and anything that could not be evaluated and understood spelt potential danger to a fox. They moved round him cautiously, keeping the same distance, sniffing, listening, forever wary of a trap.

Jack swung round with them on his painful tether, trying to keep his eyes on both with quick movements of his head, his swollen leg not forgotten but ignored under this new threat. At last the dog fox was sure there was nothing to fear from this victim and a constant stream of saliva drooled from his mouth as Jack's blood ran freer and scented the air tantalisingly. He stopped dead, body close to the ground, fangs bared ready for the kill. The vixen copied him. Jack's body quivered, not from fear but from the unmistakable tightening of the already tense atmosphere and he half crouched in an attitude of defence —the hopeless defence of a child pitted against two experienced slaughterers. The foxes had now turned their full concentration on to the job in hand and for the moment nothing existed for them except Jack and the meal he would make and all their cunning and wariness was directed at picking out the moment to attack and complete the butchery without risking even the slightest nip in return. It was this concentration of thought and instinct that was their downfall.

They should have had him killed and dragged away to the den long before another killer, seasoned as themselves, hurled his big body into the little depression to join in the drama.

Rex had tracked Jack silently and when the faint breeze had carried the tell-tale scent of his enemy, the fox, he moved slowly for he knew the merest sound would alert the slayer of game and send him bolting for cover. But when he'd seen what was taking place through the fringe of grass on the lip of the shallow hollow, he'd hurled himself at the unsuspecting back of the vixen. The dog fox was round and away with a fluid movement so fast it looked as though he'd vanished into the ground but the vixen paused a fateful split second and screamed as she was smashed to the ground by Rex's hundred and ten pounds of furious muscle and the big yellow teeth savaged into her neck. The big dog bit deeper into the spinal column, oblivious of the frantic, desperate struggles and Jack yelped and jumped about on three legs in an undreamed-of ecstasy of excitement. Quite suddenly the mother fox slumped and hung slack in Rex's grip and after one more exertion of those mighty jaws which crunched clean through the bones, he tossed the lifeless body to one side contemptuously and raised his head to bark into the night.

The answer came back so faint that human ears would have missed it, two high notes whistled through the teeth. Rex bounded away.

Jack tried to follow him but the first pull of the snare had him crying with the pain and he lay down sorrowfully to lick at the blood. He didn't have too long to wait and the earth clearly transmitted the thump of Tom's running feet before he was near enough to be seen. Rex was first back, with Tom carrying a large torch a few yards behind.

The man dropped to his knees to examine Jack in the torchlight and when he saw the cause of the injury he cursed loudly and strongly with a blaze of temper. Jack cried, thinking the hard words were meant for him, so Tom dropped his voice to a soft murmur as he took out his knife to cut the wire.

'Looks like a bloody nasty mess you've got there, Jack, me old mate. Now this might hurt a bit but I'll have to get it off your leg and I'll be as quick as I can.'

The flesh around the cut had swollen up in two ridges completely burying the wire and Tom had to lie with Jack's wriggling body under his armpit, holding his snapping head with his left hand as he probed into the raw flesh for the eye of the noose. Jack's wild attempts to break free didn't help but all the time Tom kept up a flow of soft, soothing words. At last the wire came loose and he used a clean handkerchief as a temporary bandage, picked Jack up like a baby and called Rex to heel to start the four-mile walk home. He remembered the vixen and turned back to cut off the brush with a quick stroke of his clasp knife. The carcass he left for the carrion.

It was a hard, tiring tramp over the rough ground but Tom covered the distance without stopping to rest, anxious to attend to the wound properly and see if there was likely to be any permanent damage. From the top of the last hill, the lighted kitchen window was a yellow square of welcome and at the door Agnes, in dressing gown and hair curlers, took Jack from Tom's aching arms and laid him on the table to remove the bloody handkerchief with a great deal of petting and baby talk. Jack didn't respond. He'd had enough pain for that night, and Tom had to hold him down as Agnes washed the blood away with warm water.

With her thumbs she carefully opened the wound and said, 'Looks as though his tendons aren't damaged. Good job he wasn't bigger and stronger or he'd have cut his leg in two. Whose was the snare, could you tell?'

Tom shook his head. 'No, it was one of those ready-made ones the ironmonger's sell. But I'm going to make it known that anyone I catch at it on this land in future's going to get a backside full of shot. If Rex wasn't the tracker he is, I don't think I'd have found him this week, he was right over near Pinetree Spinney.'

He had to hold Jack until Agnes had deftly bandaged his leg and then he placed the dog in his own corner where he looked sorry for himself and licked gently at the white dressing. Tom turned to Rex who was sitting under a shelf in anticipation. The old dog knew he'd worked well and the shelf held the food for the animals including a carton of chocolate drops. Tom gave him a large handful, playfully tugging at the thick ruff as the chocolates rapidly disappeared.

'You're one of the best, Rex. Let's hope a bit of you rubs off on your understudy before he gets himself killed.' He got to his feet slowly, stretching and yawning. 'I'll take Jack to the vet first thing after breakfast, and as soon as his leg's all right I'd better take him in hand, start teaching him the do's and don'ts.'

Agnes refilled Jack's drinking dish and yawned mightily herself. 'Anyway, he's learned what a fox is and that's one smell he'll never forget. Come on to bed, it's nearly half past three.'

When the light went out Jack dropped into a sleep that lasted until he was laid on the vet's table in the surgery, barely stirring when Tom carried him to the Land Rover and then from the vehicle into the vet's house.

Arthur Cawthorne was a big, bluff, loud man, bigger all round than Tom, with a genuine heartiness which went a long way to gaining the confidence of his patients. Jack licked happily at the beefy hands—until they started to unfasten the bandage; then with the pain still fresh in his mind, he tried to nip at them. But Arthur had been in his business over forty years and was wise to the ways of young dogs. He had been watching for the move and was too quick for the young teeth. After that Tom held Jack down with one large hand on his head and one on his rump. The bandage had stuck to the cut and Jack surprised them with his strength as he struggled in vain to get away.

'Steady now, you little bugger,' Arthur laughed—he laughed at almost everything. 'This doesn't hurt half as much as that snare did.'

He washed the gash clean and started to bandage it again. 'Nothing to worry about, Tom, he'll be as good as new in a week or two, doesn't even need a stitch. Bring him back next week. Just the injection now.'

Jack nearly caught them unawares when the needle went in and his previous wrigglings were nothing to the way he reacted to the hypodermic. He simply erupted and a less experienced man would have left half the needle in his flesh.

'You little sod!' Tom said as he tightened his grip on the writhing body and Arthur boomed delightedly. 'I'll tell you what, Tom, you've a dog with plenty of spirit there. That's it, let him go.'

Jack was off the table like a bullet. He ran round the room once and then seemed to forget the whole incident. He shook himself and sniffed interestedly at the strange smells coming from Arthur's well-worn tweed trousers, the scent of cows, horses and sheep all well impregnated by the vet's daily rounds of farms and smallholdings. Arthur bent to have his hand licked again and grinned. 'Anyway, he doesn't hold a grudge. That'll be one-sixty-five including vat. Rex still going strong?'

Tom put the money on the table. 'Aye, he looks like goin' on for ever although I bought Jack because the old lad's got to go sometime ... there's not many Rexes knocking about, Arthur. Still, see you in the Bull on Saturday.'

Arthur gave Jack a final pat. 'You will at that. Send the next one in, will you.'

Jack's leg healed well. He went back twice to the surgery and then was pronounced 'fit for anything'. Tom started the job of turning him into a working dog.

The first requirement for obedience was to learn to walk properly at 'heel' with his neck close to Tom's left leg. He was persuaded into doing this by the use of a chain choke-collar and a four-foot leather lead. Whenever the dog started to forge ahead of the man, a sharp tug on the lead tightened the running noose of chain around Jack's neck and jerked him back into position. The action didn't hurt Jack but the shock of having his progress halted made him think a while before he tried it again. Speed up he did, continually, but over the first few weeks Tom had to use the lead less and less.

He gave the lessons on the open grass at the side of the house each evening after tea, just fifteen-minute periods at first which were gradually increased to half an hour, so steadily that Jack never noticed. Tom made the training as much fun as possible and Jack was always ready to play.

As the summer turned to autumn the dog's efficiency grew in proportion to his sprouting body, which in turn measured up to his insatiable appetite. He was perpetually hungry and it was his greediness that brought Tom's wrath on his head for the first time.

Tom was both delighted and proud of the way Jack was coming on with the obedience and one evening when they were training, Arthur Cawthorne's car pulled up at the house and the vet came to sit on the grass beside the bored and dozing Rex, to watch.

Tom grinned at him. 'You've heard the saying, "How's that for a twelve-year-old dog?" Well, how's this for a six-month-old pup?'

He really put Jack through his paces to show off to Arthur. They did meticulous heelwork both on and off the lead with Tom marching about like a soldier and Jack glued to his proper position throughout a series of right, left and about turns. Jack sat or lay still for minutes on end with Tom out of sight, and he came hurrying in to sit upright, looking up at Tom when he was recalled from a distance. He did a perfect retrieve with a training dumb-bell, a light wooden copy of those weightlifters use, and dropped flat at the first command wherever he was or whatever he was doing. Tom could send him away and drop him on any given spot within reasonable distance.

When they'd gone through the repertoire Arthur raised his eyebrows. 'By hell, Tom, you've put some work in with him haven't you?'

Tom was beaming. 'Not as much as you'd think—only normal—but he's a bright little bugger all right. I've never seen an animal learn so quick. Been thinking o' taking him out with us now, get him used to the sheep and cattle up on the grazing round Bracken Crag. He doesn't see much livestock round here.'

Arthur nodded. 'It'd be as well. You don't want him shot for sheep worrying the first time you let him off the lead.'

Tom asked him into the house for a cup of tea and a sandwich and Arthur heaved himself off the ground.

'Thought you was never goin' to ask. That's what I came for. My missus has gone to London with the Women's Institute and I'm a lousy cook so I'm cadging a meal here and there when I can.'

Jack and Rex preceded them round the house to the kitchen as they followed slowly, chatting.

'The wife'll soon whip up a salad for you if you don't mind a bit of cold duck,' Tom offered.

'If there's one thing designed to make a man's mouth water, it's cold duck salad,' Arthur, who was extremely fond of his large belly, accepted.

Tom went in first. 'Agnes! Can you give Arthur something to eat, he's ...'

Arthur bumped into Tom's back as he stopped unexpectedly and stared disbelievingly into Jack's corner. Arthur wasn't the only one who appreciated cold duck. Jack was lying on the floor holding the remains of the bird with his front paws, stripping off the last of the meat before he started on the bones. Tom's neck reddened and his bushy eyebrows came down in what his family knew as a sure sign of menace about to explode.

Arthur looked over Tom's shoulder and said with badly concealed delight, 'What did you say he is, a Belgian Duckhound?'

Tom bellowed, *'Jack, leave!'* just as Agnes came through from the front of the house. She glanced from her husband's pop-eyed expression to Arthur's big grinning face and to the object of Tom's wrath who was unconcernedly starting on the ribs.

'Oh dear,' she murmured, but the corners of her wide mouth were twitching.

'Well trained dog, that,' Arthur said affably, unable to resist rubbing it in a little.

She started to say, 'This is the first time ...' when Tom almost screamed, '*Jack, leave!*'

Jack looked up apprehensively with the carcass firmly in his mouth, beginning to get the idea that he was in bad books but without the slightest intention of leaving his delicious snack for anyone. Further words refused to come from Tom's apopleptic throat at this show of direct disobedience and he rushed violently across the kitchen. He wasn't quick enough. Jack darted away, showing he knew he was guilty of something by the way he slunk under the table with his head carried low and his ears flat back. Tom chased him from the table to ribald advice from Arthur and pleas from Agnes not to be too rough, and trapped him in a corner. Jack held grimly on to his booty, watching Tom approach from the corner of his eyes. When Tom reached down to take it from him he tried to bolt again but he wasn't quick enough this time and Tom grabbed two handfuls of his ruff, which was getting fairly long, stood him on his hind legs and swung him energetically from side to side as he yelled a stream of threats into his ear.

'*When I tell you to leave, you leave, Jack De Bloody Montpelier or you'll be finishing up inside a tin of dog food instead of the other way about. Leave it, leave it, leave it!*'

This was Jack's first real taste of chastisement and he was frightened, much more than hurt, by the bawling voice and after a few seconds of being an animated pendulum he opened his jaws and let the chewed-up remains of the duck fall to the floor. Both Agnes and Arthur were well acquainted with Tom's highly successful methods of dog training but an uninitiated person would have been surprised to see his Jekyll and Hyde character in operation. The instant Jack carried out the order to 'leave' Tom was all love and affection, rubbing his hands into the maturing coat, laughing and praising.

'That's a *good* dog, you're a *good* lad, aren't you, Jack?'

As Arthur had remarked the first time he'd met him, Jack wasn't one to bear a grudge. He sat, mouth open, tongue lolling, basking in the warmth of Tom's petting and when Tom told him to stay, with the tattered duck three feet away on the floor, he stayed.

Tom said to Arthur, 'And that, laughing boy, is a little lesson for you in how to handle a dog. No matter how bad they've been, make a fuss of 'em when they do what you've told 'em.'

'And I suppose,' Arthur answered, still grinning and working on the variations of the incident with which he'd regale his cronies at the Bull Hotel, 'he'll never pinch another bit of meat as long as he lives.'

'Oh, he'll do that all right till he's a bit older, but he'll learn, he'll learn.'

Agnes went to the fridge. 'How about some pork pie, Arthur?'

'The thing I love best next to duck is pork pie, Agnes love, with a few peas and mint sauce.'

Tom prodded Arthur's rotund middle. 'The thing Arthur Cawthorne likes best next to *anything* to eat, is *anything* to eat—*STAY!*'

Left to his own devices Jack had his neck stretched out to suck up the tantalising smell of the duck but at Tom's shout he snapped back to the proper sitting position.

'That's a good dog,' Tom carolled. 'We'll show this horse doctor who's the best dog in the country, won't we?'

'Better than Rex?'

'Well,' Tom amended, 'the best *young* dog in the country, anyway.'

'Mmmm,' Arthur said with deliberate scepticism, 'I've a fiver says he doesn't win a novice event this year.'

That didn't give Tom much time to prepare Jack as no dogs under six months are allowed to be entered in a Kennel Club show and Jack wouldn't be eligible until October and there weren't many shows held after that until the spring. But Tom was always ready to put his money where his mouth was.

He nodded. 'You're on. Jack! Go in your corner and get some rest, you're going to need it.'

Jack went with one more longing look at the duck and an expression that could only be described as one of regret.

Chapter 3

(3)

The intensifying of Jack's training programme coincided with the start of the second period of his life; going out to work. He now had an obedience lesson before breakfast as well as the one in the evening and he was out on the estate all day with Tom and Rex, constantly being called under command and he took to the life as though he had been born to it, which he may well have been.

For the first few days Tom kept him on the lead, knowing the new surroundings would claim his attention and make it hard for Tom to hold it. The first time Jack saw a flock of sheep at the northern end of the estate where the lush southern slopes of Bracken Hill, which was topped by the black mass of Bracken Crag, were rented out as grazing land to the local sheep farmers, he nearly went berserk. Dragging at the lead, he whined and snapped as though it were his first day out of the kennels. Tom kept him at a distance for the first two days until he got used to the smell and had calmed down a little. Then gradually he took him in closer, a few yards nearer each day until they were right in amongst the sheep and Jack was able to sniff and examine the strange creatures to his heart's content; the novelty soon wore off. Tom went there every day until he was sure Jack was fully accustomed to them, and then he did the same with a herd of cows which fed on the banks of the river on the western boundary of the estate. When Jack was at ease with the cattle Tom said, 'Now you know who you've *not* got to harm I'll have to try to introduce you to the villains of the place.'

But first he introduced him to Ned White, one of his two assistants who worked on the estate. Ned lived in the north-east corner of the property, near the road, with his wife and son. Ned was a forester and the care of the stands of trees, the cutting for sale as lumber and replanting were in his hands. He also kept the dams and weirs and boundary fences in good repair and otherwise helped out in any way he could.

His colleague, Ira Love, had an ancient cottage close to the river in the west, about four miles away and he was a gamekeeper of the old school who asked for no more than a stretch of open country with all its inhabitants to tuck under his wing to mother. Into his province, too, came the trout and salmon streams, four of them and he was famed for his uncanny knack of materialising on the banks of the streams the instant an illicit line or net was cast, whatever the time of day or night. Few and far between were those intrepid enough to venture on to Scargill estate property with rod, snare or gun. There were a few, as proved by Jack's misadventure, but the amount of game they succeeded in poaching was negligible.

Ned was tall and thin with a zest for life and fun which belied his solemn, lugubrious countenance but he was as ruthless as Ira with 'rabbit rustlers', as he called poachers, and didn't hesitate to report his long-time partner in the dominoes team of the Bull when he caught him with a full bag early one morning.

He was working on the teeth of the mobile circular saw with a triangular saw file when Tom drove into the yard and he whistled up his own Border Collie who was nearly as old as Rex but indecently fat due to Mrs White's kind heart and liberal nature with titbits.

'Geordie,' Ned said seriously as his dog waddled up, 'you'd better get pally with your new gaffer.'

To Jack, who had tired of trying to get Rex to play chasing games, the Collie was a would-be playmate who wouldn't growl grumpily at the invitation to come and run. After a tentative smelling by both parties Jack darted about quickly in front of Geordie's nose in an attempt to get him interested. Geordie watched him with his head on one side, yawned, stretched and lay down in the dust.

'You're wasting your time, Jack,' Tom grinned. 'You've more chance getting Rex to play than old lightning here.'

'Hey,' Ned said, 'less of the insults or I'll turn him loose on you.'

'You'd have to prise him up off the ground. How about a cup of tea?'

They went into the house, chatting, while Jack went exploring. He found a big barn with a tractor parked next to an old cart and the inevitable chickens and ducks, and was about to go and make a final assault on Geordie's better nature when a new, strange smell drifted towards him. It was a strong smell, as strong as a fox's, but different although no less intriguing. The scent was coming on the breeze from somewhere behind the barn and Jack set off at a full run to trace it. He skidded round the corner and stopped dead, looking at an animal he'd never seen before. It was a thin, scrawny, dirty white specimen with a straggly beard, a pair of curved horns and the most unfriendly eyes. It was tearing the longish grass from the foot of the barn wall and chomping stolidly. When it heard Jack, its head turned to glare a baleful warning at the upstart and then went back to its feeding. Jack didn't recognise the threat, moving cautiously closer, head stretched out, sniffing rapidly at the pungent odour. When ten feet separated them, the goat turned its head again and snorted, giving the interloper a last warning and Jack, as if catching on he wasn't going to get the red carpet of welcome, dropped flat on his belly. The goat carried on feeding.

Having been given his inch, permission to watch, Jack wanted his yard, close contact for a thorough examination. Bunching his hind-legs under his body, he slithered, still flat to the ground, a foot nearer, then another, and again until he'd halved the distance. The goat watched his insidious progress obliquely, deigning not to turn his full attention on this stripling who'd dared to encroach on his territory until it was time to assert his authority. But when the goat had deemed Jack had had more than his share of tolerance it acted so quickly that it nearly caught the dog unawares. One stiff-legged jump had it facing the object of its displeasure and, with a whistling snort, the head was lowered as it started to charge. Jack could get to his feet quickly enough when the need arose but he only just managed to twist sideways and miss a buffetting that would have caved in his ribs. The goat's fore-hooves dug into the dirt as it skidded into a cat-like turn and started a second charge without a pause. Jack was willing to play the chasing game with anyone or anything but something told him this wasn't the game according to his rules and if he didn't take off smartly he'd have a good chance of ending the day back on the vet's table. In the classic canine manner he stuck his tail between his legs and bolted.

The goat was neither slow nor of a forgiving nature and with Jack's posterior firmly in its sights it tore after him on a full circuit of the barn and then across the yard.

Ned's poultry were allowed to roam at will during daylight hours and were contentedly scratching and pecking for worms and other such delicacies when their peaceful existence was shattered by a thunderbolt, followed closely by another, which appeared amongst them as if from nowhere. Like the shock waves of a bomb they panicked in all directions, squawking raucously with a great deal of useless wing-flapping. Rex got up from where he was snoozing beside the Land Rover, to see what the commotion was about but dropped down again with an expression of disgust when he saw it was only his frivolous subordinate. Even Geordie raised his head, albeit very briefly, at the rumpus but there were very few things on earth now that could stir him, certainly not a reckless pup being chased by a goat.

Ned went to the window, took one look and made for the door. 'Hell, Tom, I forgot that bad-tempered old sod, Mephistopheles. He'll tupp your dog over the roof if he catches him.'

When they got out into the yard, Jack had done an adroit about-turn and was racing back towards them. And when he saw Tom, he changed direction again to run to him for protection. Jack had increased his lead and Mephistopheles was now ten yards behind. When he ran round behind Tom's legs Ned jumped in front of the goat shouting and waving his arms and the animated battering ram ploughed to a thwarted stop.

'Go on, you black hearted old bugger,' Ned yelled. 'Away.'

The goat stood his ground for a moment or two to show he wasn't afraid, then walked slowly and grudgingly back to the barn. Jack bravely came from behind Tom's legs as if to start it all again.

'Sit!' Tom said, 'You've caused enough trouble and you'd better start learning who to tease and who not to tease or you're going to cost me a fortune in vet's fees.'

'You're a poet and don't know it,' Ned grinned.

Jack was shut in the Land Rover for the rest of the visit

and he didn't think much of that at all; he still hadn't had a good sniff at the goat from close quarters.

The next day they went to see Ira Love and were just in time to catch him as he was leaving with his shotgun under his arm. When he saw them coming down the track he went back into his cottage and had a bottle of beer ready poured for Tom. He was cutting thick slices of bread from a fat, home-baked loaf, spreading them liberally with butter and sandwiching rough cut pieces of beef between each pair. He was an imperturbable, stocky man from the Norfolk Fens with a red-brown face and purple nose. He too was a regular visitor at the Bull and it was said the only liquid to pass his mouth was the brown frothy kind which comes in pint bottles.

He didn't turn from his job when Tom entered the room, saying in his East Anglian accent, 'Better have a bite, Tom. Found otter tracks up by the big pool last night. We'll have to see if we can't catch him.'

The salmon were running and one otter could do an awful lot of damage to the game fish. A pair of otters, mates, would merrily kill dozens in the love play, showing off to each other by taking a single bite from each fish and leaving it to perish in its own time. Tom had seen the surface of that same big pool littered with corpses on two occasions and with the number of salmon rivers being dwindled down with pollution, the ones that were still in a swimmable state had to be protected more than ever against thieves, human or otherwise. Ira knew there was no need to ask Tom for help—nothing would keep him away from the stream until the otter had been caught or they knew for sure it had been chased out of the district.

Tom took a mouthful of beer. 'Has it done much damage?'

Ira wrapped the food in a piece of old oilcloth. 'Few trout's all I found, but give him time. There weren't many tracks an' it looks like he be a newcomer. Be a different tale today, I'm thinking.'

'Do you know which holt it's using?'

'No, but Dapper'll smell him out.'

At the mention of the name an unkempt mongrel, which was largely Old English Sheepdog by the length of its coat, came from under the table to have his ears rubbed.

Tom said, 'I've got my young dog with me, maybe we'd better leave him here. He gets a bit excited and he might spoil things.'

Ira poured his beer into his mouth quickly and it seemed to find its own way down his throat without the aid of any swallowing.

'Naw, don't do that. How's he goin' to learn anything if you keeps him at home. He'll be all right on the lead till he feels his way.'

Jack, as usual, was first to bound from the Land Rover when Tom let them out, with Rex following at a more sane pace. The men gave Jack and Dapper a minute or two to get to know each other while Tom got his gun and ammunition from the car and then they set off north up the river bank.

The big pool had been made by damming one of the estate streams, a tributary of the river, and the low wall of the dam made a perfect salmon leap. It was a good hour's walk from Ira's cottage and the easiest and flattest way was to follow the river to where the stream emptied and then follow the stream.

The two men walked together, Tom with Jack fretfully on the lead. The older dogs were loose to roam and forage at will and he wanted to be with them.

'No good you carrying on like that, lad, you'll get your turn all in good time,' Tom told him.

Jack wasn't pacified, he kept inching out in front of Tom almost to the extent of the lead, to be jerked back to heel time and again. They passed four men casting flies for trout and salmon and away to the east in a large thicket a shotgun boomed twice in quick succession.

Ira spat. 'That Right Honourable somebody or another's wasted his money ain't he? I'll bet he can't hit one o' the trees, never mind a rising pheasant.'

Tom snatched Jack back again. 'Can't say I'm sorry, if everyone who took a licence out was as bad a shot as he is there'd be a lot more birds left for the Christmas market.'

A large part of the estate's income came from the table birds sold to hotels for the festive season along with salmon and trout. Ducks, chickens and eggs went to the market all year round and the occasional order for venison with the fees for shooting and fishing rights added to the interest from the trust fund, kept the Scargill estate finances in a sound, healthy position. But of course the amount of game that could be taken was restricted and every marksman who wasn't as good as he imagined himself to be, left more birds to fall to the guns of Tom and Ira.

They turned from the river to follow the smaller watercourse with Rex and Dapper splashing happily through the shallows, sending basking fish darting for the safety of deep water, and Jack getting more and more excited and less and less enchanted at being confined to the limit of the length of the lead. The stream was about twenty-five feet wide with low banks at this point and thick clusters of oak and beech crowding close to the water. The path was narrow and walled in by a mass of bushes and brambles growing under the trees.

Ira said, 'Be as well to let him have a run before we get up to the big pool, should be safe enough here, he can't do no harm.'

'I don't know,' Tom hesitated, 'he's coming on champion

at home where there's no distractions but I haven't forgotten that fox he went after.'

'Well, you'll have to find out sooner or later if you can recall him in all conditions.'

Ira was the acknowledged authority on all animals, dogs in particular, in the district and he was right, Jack could hardly take off for the open country through that dense undergrowth. Tom slipped the choker over his head. 'Away, Jack.'

Jack went. Backwards and forwards along the bank, recognising the criss-cross scent of rabbits and picking up others that were new to him. He behaved more like a beagle, moving quickly, nose to the ground in fast little runs, changing direction often. He was oblivious to everything except the all-consuming trails of which there were so many intersecting others he barely moved five yards on one before another crossed it and he was off on that one.

The men walked on slowly with Rex and Dapper now far ahead and when Jack had had ten minutes' freedom Tom decided to test him.

'Come, Jack,' he shouted—the accepted recall command—standing straight, feet together in the approved manner of the obedience trials ring to which Jack was accustomed. Jack should have happily run to his master and stopped in a sitting position close up to his legs, attentively awaiting the next command as he'd done hundreds of times before in the training sessions. This time Jack simply didn't want to know. He heard the shout all right but acted as though he hadn't, carrying on with his feverish, aimless tracking without a pause. Tom didn't move. Now the order had been given Jack would have to be made to obey it even if it took all day. Ned sat on a log, stuffing his pipe patiently and Tom's voice cracked out again, *'Come, Jack!'*

He got the same response as before and shouted again and Jack still wasn't having any so Tom had to recourse to a method slightly less satisfactory but for some reason often more successful, *'Down!'* he bellowed, *'Down!'*

It may be that to drop flat in the vicinity that had taken the dog's fancy was a less disagreeable order than the recall but whatever the reason Jack lay down and that was Tom's thin end of the wedge. Having gained full attention he called, 'Come, Jack,' and Jack came as desired.

Ned puffed his pipe. 'Sweet as a nut, Tom, he's like all the young 'uns.'

Tom ruffled Jack's ears and gave him a few more minutes running as a reward.

'Away.'

Jack took off after Rex and Dapper but still acting like a Bloodhound with his nose missing the ground only fractionally. Tom took the knapsack from the ground where Ned had laid it to enjoy his smoke—a knapsack heavy with food of the bottled variety as well as doorstep sandwiches—swung it across his shoulder and started to follow the dogs.

Two hundred yards upstream was the start of the white water where the banks narrowed and the stream rushed over the first of the weirs. Beyond the weir the banks widened and flattened again into a peaceful miniature lake. The weir was four feet high and an easy leap for a fifteen or twenty pound fighting gamefish and as Jack paused to look and listen at the small waterfall, one of the big silvery visitors from the Atlantic shot eight feet into the air, a flash of curved grace, to drop tail first into the still water above the fall. Jack's head thrust forward, his body half crouched ready for defence or attack. Seconds after, another shiny fish arched upwards to disappear tail first beneath the smooth, grey surface. It was too much for Jack. He barked twice, ignoring the shout of *'Down,*

Jack!', accelerated as much as possible on the short run afforded by the bank and hurled himself after the fish.

He hadn't thought about the water or the consequences of jumping into it, all he knew was he had to catch the large, legless beast that could jump higher than he could. He did think about the water when it closed shockingly over his head and filled his nostrils and he found it wasn't still at all but was rushing at great speed and sweeping him helplessly towards the weir. He choked and stopped breathing when the force of the current flattened him against the weir wall three feet below the surface. He'd never swum before but instinctively his legs paddled madly upwards with the force of the water pressing him against the wall impeding his progress. He didn't give in to the drag of the rough stone on his coat, he knew the only way to survive was to go upwards but just before he broke the surface he had to relieve his burning lungs and dragged in a gulp of water. The power of the water which had nearly drowned him, now helped him as it pushed his head and one shoulder over the waterfall. The first thing he did was retch to clear his lungs, then he hung where he was with the white foam churning around him, gasping in sweet air such as he'd never breathed before.

'Jack, Jack.' Tom was knee-deep in the stream clapping his hands and beckoning. 'Come, Jack! Come on, lad, you can do it. Come on, that's a good boy.'

The brief experience with an unknown quantity had startled the dog and he desperately wanted to get back to a quantity he did know; Tom. If it hadn't been so dangerous, his method of progress would have been comic. With his right leg hanging over the weir and waving uselessly he scrambled madly, half swimming, half crawling across the force of the torrent. He didn't stop to rest, wanting to get away from this grip that wasn't really a grip, urged on and encouraged by Tom and Ira.

Tom reached out, holding on to Ira's shotgun, to pull him the last few feet and lift him on to the bank. If the men had expected to get in any resuscitation practice, they were out of luck. The instant his feet touched the earth, Jack shook himself vigorously and set off upstream to look for more salmon.

This time, he heard and obeyed. *'Down!'*

He lay panting as Tom came up and put the choker round his neck, scolding gently, 'Do you know how much money I paid for you, dog? And that's the second time you've nearly got yourself done in. The quicker you learn to do what you're told, the safer you're going to be.'

They called in the other dogs now they were getting quite close to the big pool and the place where Ira had found the otter tracks. Farther up, the stream narrowed again and the second weir came in sight with the big pool behind it. This man-made lake was about three hundred yards long and perhaps seventy wide with a small island at the upper end. Two men in waders were casting flies from the shallow water at the far side.

Ira inclined his head at them. 'If we don't shift that otter quick, they'll be complainin' you've sold them licences under false pretences. There'll be nothin' left for them to catch. Here's the track, see—and some fresh 'uns since last night.'

In the soft sandy soil close to the water, the long dragmark of the powerful rudder was unmistakable.

'Which holt you reckon he's in?' Tom asked.

'There's three old ones in this pool and he'll be likely to use the nearest one to him when he gets tired. We'll start with the nearest to us.'

A few yards away the bank rose in a hump which overhung the water and the entrance to the holt which was half in, half out of the water and invisible from the bank.

The men stood, one on either side of the hump of ground, shotguns loaded and ready, not that they really expected an otter to leave the water in daylight when he was being hunted. Ira bent to touch the tracks and Dapper came up to sniff them and when Ira said, 'Seek', Dapper knew the drill. He was an old hand at otter hunting and, like Ira, knew every holt on the estate.

Tom tied Jack to a sapling and stood ready with Rex at his side. Dapper plunged into the water, swimming out of sight under the undercut bank. The water was four feet deep at the mouth of the holt but very clear with a bottom of sand and pebbles so if the fish thief was there and bolted they'd at least catch a glimpse of him. It only took Dapper a few minutes to find that the dark cave with its sleeping ledge was empty.

When he'd shaken the wet from his long coat, they set off for the next one, opposite the island. This one wasn't as good as the first from the otter's point of view. It had two entrances, both narrow gaps between the twisted roots of an old oak, the water having cut the soil away from the foot of the tree and leaving it in a seemingly precarious position, but both doorways were above water level and this was the one Tom hoped the otter had chosen to use that morning.

When Jack was tied safely to a bush the men took an entrance each with Rex midway between them, the shallow water barely halfway up his legs. Ira took Dapper up to the right-hand hole.

'Fetch him, fetch him.'

The opening was only just wide enough for the dog to squeeze through but with a heave his rump disappeared into the blackness. They heard him bark at once: he'd found the otter. Now, much depended on the geography of the holt. The otter's home would be a labyrinth of tunnels threading amongst the downthrusting great roots and there would almost surely be passages too small for Dapper to get through but the otter's fear of the dog and the men he knew would be waiting for him, might drive him to try for the water where nothing would catch him.

The fox has a well-earned name for cunning but the otter can be, as many a farmer would testify, equally crafty and like foxes grow more artful with experience. This otter was an old one and well versed in the ways of men and their dogs. Two seasons earlier he had prepared another exit from this holt in a place men would never look; on the other side of the tree away from the water. He knew both exits they expected him to use would be sealed off and could lead only to death, and as the hated dog scent came closer in the darkness he bared his sharp teeth and turned round to do the unexpected. Dapper heard him moving and barked furiously, deafeningly in the confined space, searching frantically for a way into the sleeping chamber but the tunnels were too small for him.

Outside the men waited patiently, knowing that if the otter could be driven out Dapper could do it, and if he couldn't, they'd resort to smoke and get him out anyway.

Ira said, 'I keep meaning to get a terrier, a Cairn or ...'

He meant a dog smaller than an otter that could go in anywhere an otter could, but Jack's yelping and the threshing of the bush as he lunged to break loose had Tom scrambling up the bank. As he looked over the top the otter was streaking away, his black whiskered face turning back over his shoulder, watching for pursuit.

'Rex!' Tom shouted and flung up his gun for one hasty shot which missed; then the otter was out of range, running on a curve which would take him back to the water. Tom pointed downstream and shouted urgently, 'Away. Fetch!'

Rex raced along the top of the bank, not knowing why

he was being sent until he caught sight of the black shiny coat speeding close to the ground. Rex barked for sheer joy of the hunt and lengthened his stride, lacking the speed of his younger days but still with the stamina-packed muscles that would get him to the bottom end of the big pool before the otter.

In the holt Dapper was finding his way out of the maze of tunnels in answer to Ira's repeated shouts of recall, barking and whining alternately in his eagerness to get in the chase. The fishermen across the pool had climbed the bank to see what was going on and from their grandstand view cheered and urged on Rex.

Jack was going wild. The otter had flashed within six feet of him, leaving on the still air the warm scent of a mammal mingled with the smell of fishy breath. Time after time Jack hurled himself to the extent of the lead, trying to break loose and follow the most exciting trail he'd yet come across and that included the fox's. This was a golden opportunity for his education and Tom didn't let it pass but before being freed Jack had to be brought under control. Control and obedience were to be the cornerstones of his life.

'Sit!' Tom commanded.

Jack flung himself out on the restricting lead again.

'*Down!*' Tom literally screamed.

Jack didn't drop flat but he hesitated and in the pause Tom bent to his ear. '*Get down!*'

Jack lowered his belly down, not willingly, but the important thing was he did it. Tom said, 'Sit!'

Jack sat with alacrity.

'Good boy. Stay!'

This was the crucial test. Tom slowly removed the choker from Jack's neck, ready to grab his ruff if he tried to take off before being ordered. The dog was trembling and leaning so far forward he could hardly be said to be in a proper sitting position, but he stayed. Tom kept him there a few seconds, then, 'Away, Jack.' Jack went like a bullet.

Of course he hadn't the finesse, the know-how of Rex, he didn't consider the course of the otter and the best way to cut him off; the fact that the shortest distance between two points is a straight line he had yet to learn and he was guided by his instinct alone. The only way for Jack was to follow that unforgettable fish taint on the air and he moved on the otter's tracks, in a deep curve. Dapper bounded up the bank and sat to wait for Ira who was scrambling up somewhat slower. The men paused a moment to take in the situation.

It was plain that Rex was going to stop the otter reaching the water and it wouldn't be long before the otter realised it and took some other action and his most probable strategy would be to try to get across country to the south where the second of the estate streams flowed down to the river a quarter of a mile below Ira's cottage. Ira pointed Dapper's head to the south-west, at an angle of about forty-five degrees to the stream.

'Away, Dapper!'

Dapper went off fast in a dead straight line and the men moved off at an angle between Dapper and the line of the stream.

The three dogs were now closing the otter in a triangle, or would be when Dapper got into position, and the otter began to realise that all was not well. He saw Rex racing parallel to his own course and with flashing backward glances picked out Jack closing the avenue of retreat to his rear. Not that he would have gone that way. The guns were that way and as fearsome as the dogs were he'd sooner chance his luck with them than the roaring shotguns, against which he had no defence at all. His first mate had died a sudden death when they had been on a chicken raid at a lonely farm. The only way open to him was to turn left and make for the south stream, just as Ira had guessed, and as distasteful as it was to run away from his beloved safe water, he had no option. Like a cat he twisted and changed direction without losing speed. Now he was travelling directly away from Rex and across Jack's path.

The anglers across the water cheered again and at a whistle and wave of the arm from Tom, Rex ran directly after the quarry. Dapper was nearly where Ira wanted him and Ira said, 'Looks as though your young feller's goin' to get blooded if I know anything about otters.'

Tom grunted, anxious now and half sorry he'd let Jack go. 'Let's hope he's the fighting sort of dog he's supposed to be.'

Ira put his fingers to his mouth and whistled twice. Dapper turned right and made the third angle of the triangle with the otter squarely in the centre and all three dogs were closing fast. Ira had been right again. The otter knew which was the youngest and therefore weakest and most inexperienced of his foes, and he turned again to the left, straight at Jack, with teeth bared ready to fight for his life and sell it dearly if he had to die. But he knew no fear yet, he'd been in tight corners before and had lived to pass on some of his cunning to his cubs. He intended to get out of this one, too.

The otter was holding his own with Rex and Dapper as far as speed goes but the distance from him to Jack was diminishing rapidly and his confidence grew when he was close enough to see just how young was the only bar to his freedom. Not much more than half grown, nowhere near his own weight or sinewy strength and wasting his breath on unseemly yelping instead of saving it for the chase and the fight. He knew, from sad experience, that he was out of range of the guns and one slash of his vicious teeth would be enough to settle the dog cub and then he would be away down to the other stream to an impregnable holt he knew of to finish his sleep and wait for the night's hunting. He looked back without lessening his speed to see that the old dogs, who were beginning to flag a little, were a good two hundred yards away. He turned his attention to Jack.

Jack didn't know what had made him want to run after the otter any more than he knew why he'd chased the fox and didn't give a thought to what would happen when they collided, which they were surely going to do. The scent of the short-legged black animal with whiskers like a cat and a queer humping gait, simply drew him like a magnet and all Tom's coaxing and chiding couldn't have pulled him off. He didn't see Rex and Dapper coming up from behind, he couldn't hear the distant cheering of the two fishermen, he was blind and deaf to all things but the otter and when he was close enough, twenty yards, to see the glinting eyes and white pointed teeth he gave one final yelp that was his war cry and drove himself at the black face.

The otter had intended to swerve at the last moment and avoid the delay of even the brief time it would take to put this young dog down but he misjudged Jack's speed and as he turned his flank, Jack's head and left shoulder crashed into his side with the comparative power of a sixteen stone rugby forward. The otter's turn had put him off balance but in the split second of contact, by a pure reflex action, he had made one raking snap and as he was flung away he had the taste of blood in his mouth. The quick bite brought a different yelp from Jack, the equivalent of a cry of pain mixed with anger, and it was suddenly clear why he had wanted to catch this animal. He wanted to bite back. He wanted to be the one to cause pain.

Jack didn't lose his footing, he turned like lightning as his slightly stunned enemy was rolling to his feet, and rushed in to have his bite. He didn't know where to bite or what he was biting, blindly closing his teeth and squeezing his jaws. The otter hissed his fury, hurling himself away and leaving Jack holding a piece of his loose neck skin. The unaccustomed taste of fresh blood of an enemy acted on Jack as though he had been suddenly whipped and he dived back into the fight, again not giving the otter time to regain his balance.

This time the nearest thing to him was the black rump and he snapped his teeth into the thick base of the rudder. It was a bad mistake. The agile, almost snake like body doubled in two and the otter's jaws locked into Jack's thigh, but Jack, in his first experience of blood lust, was above recognising pain. Even when the needle teeth cut through to his thigh bone it only acted as a goad and he clamped his own down harder into the rudder. The otter was first to let go, hissing and whistling with the agony. He twisted his rubbery body in a mad contortion to get at a more vulnerable spot and was just about to rip at Jack's soft belly when a large, grey body crashed down on top of him and a pair of jaws well used to the job took him by the throat and closed his windpipe. The otter's body jerked and twisted in convulsions of panic but he never stopped the struggle, a dog on either end of him and his position hopeless, until his oxygen-starved heart pumped its last beat and he lay still. He had died under the rules by which he had lived his long life; the rules of the hunt and no quarter given or expected.

The instant the otter's life was snuffed out a very old and very weary Rex flopped down panting, mouth hanging open, tongue lolling. Dapper ambled close to inspect the kill from a professional point of view and wondered why the pup was still hanging on to the dead otter's tail instead of licking the steadily oozing blood from his own back and thigh.

Jack was in a heaven of contentment. He didn't know the otter was dead, he didn't know what death was, but something told him the predator no longer constituted a threat and quite understandably thought himself responsible. He sighed, relaxed his jaws and for the first time felt the rising throb from his leg. He had just started to lick away the blood which was pulsing quickly from the wound when Tom and Ira ran up.

'Christ,' Tom said. 'Stay Jack, stay. Let's get him strapped up before he bleeds to death.'

They used their handkerchiefs, the strap from Ira's knapsack and strips of the oilcloth in which the sandwiches were wrapped, to cover the wound and bind Jack's hind legs together. With Jack across his shoulders, like a shepherd carrying a lamb, Tom set off by the nearest route for the Land Rover, leaving Ira to come with the dogs when they'd regained their strength.

Chapter 4

(4)

It was out of surgery hours and Arthur Cawthorne let Tom take his burden in the side door. He shook his head.

'What the hell's up now? That pup certainly knows how to get himself into trouble.'

Tom went straight through into the surgery and laid Jack on the table. 'An old dog otter, he dived in and had a go on his own, didn't you, Jack.'

He held Jack's head as Arthur started to unwrap the crude bandages. With that professional speed which can be mistaken for callousness, the vet quickly unravelled the oilcloth, the haversack strap and dropped them with the blood sodden handkerchiefs into a pedal bin. With his legs free, Jack tried to struggle to his feet, scattering blood drops all over the table and floor. They had to hold him down all the time Arthur was swabbing the wound dry to have a closer look.

He clicked his tongue. 'Deep, but by the way he's fighting there's no real damage done. Three or four stitches'll put him right.'

Even with a young, energetic, unwilling animal to hold down, it didn't take Arthur long to sew up the wound and cover it with a mass of bandages and adhesive tape.

'There y'are,' he said. 'I'll just inject him and he'll be as good as new but if you want to call that bet off it's all right. You're going to have to keep him quiet for a few days, keep him inside, no running about.'

Tom put his arms round Jack, holding him firmly to the table as Arthur filled the hypodermic.

'No, it's still on. I don't get all that many chances of taking money off you and ...' Jack bucked and heaved as the needle went in and it took all Tom's weight to hold him down.

Arthur grinned. 'You'll put him off fighting if he gets the idea it's always followed by a visit to me and a needle in his backside.'

Tom let go and Jack scrambled from the table, his injury forgotten in his haste to get away from Arthur's ministrations and he limped quickly round the room looking for an exit. Tom paid the fee and put the choker over Jack's head.

'He'll be all right when he gets a bit older and at least he's proved he's not a coward.'

That evening at Scargill Croft Jack was the hero. Tom lost count of the times he had to tell his children every detail of the adventure, how Jack had bowled the otter over and gone for the wrong end of him and Jack was cossetted, petted and fed all kinds of titbits behind Tom's back but the climax came at feeding time. Occasionally Rex was given a skinned and gutted but otherwise whole rabbit for his dinner but this evening Tom skinned two out in the yard. Rex carried his away possessively to his corner and Jack sat expectantly for his dish of minced meat to which his evening meal had been raised. Tom chopped the second rabbit in two.

'You grew up a bit today, Jack, so just for once you can have a real dog's dinner.' He dropped the hind, meaty half of the rabbit at Jack's feet. 'There y'are, let's see what you make o' that.'

Jack sniffed it, licked it, then bellied down to eat it.

He'd never tasted anything so wonderful and thrilled to the crunch of the meat encased bones. His minced meat would have been gone in the time it took him to dispose of one leg but for once he was in no hurry to devour everything in sight, lying with his meat between his paws and chewing each torn off mouthful until every drop of juice had been extracted and each small bone pulverised. That was the first time he didn't lick his own dish clean and sit looking with great longing at Rex's. When he'd finished, absolutely replete, he lapped a few times at his water, dropped his head to his paws and went to sleep.

Usually Jack was the first to wake up in the Ewing household and make a dawn tour of inspection of the kitchen floor in the vain hope of finding something edible, but the next morning he yelped with the pain of his stiffened leg as he tried to spring to his feet, having forgotten his injury. He dropped down again to find out the cause. He remembered the fight and the visit to the vet's but could only think it was the white, tight bandage that was hurting him so he started to remove it.

He started methodically at the top of his thigh gripping and tearing with his teeth, finding some of it came away easily while some of it was sticky with an unpleasant taste; this took all the growing strength of his neck and shoulders to pull loose. But he didn't give up. Gradually he got down to the lint which came away easily but got stuck in his mouth and after the lint, the evil tasting cream which the vet had rubbed directly on to the wound. He was licking off the last of the cream, preparatory to starting on the little black knots of the stitches, when the door opened and Tom came in, yawning and stretching.

He turned on the light, and started to give his cheerful greeting, 'Wakey-wakey you two ... you little sod, Jack, leave, *leave*.'

Jack was surrounded by white, whispy shreds and he

looked up alarmed at Tom's shout, the voice he used when Jack had done something wrong. Jack couldn't see what wrong he'd done this time, but he must have erred in some respect so he dropped his chin to the floor and looked up from the corners of his eyes.

Tom knelt beside him, sighing. 'I don't know what we're going to do with you, I don't. Agnes!' he shouted.

Agnes rushed in as though she expected the kitchen to be on fire, rebuttoning her night dress. Tom beckoned to her, 'Look at this.'

She bent to caress Jack's head and let him know that Tom was all bluster. 'Well, what do you expect? I'll have to talk to Arthur Cawthorne about using his brains. Any pup will pull any bandage off, if it can. Fetch me your razor and the roll of broad Elastoplast.'

'What're you going to do?'

'I'll show you.'

She rummaged about in one of the kitchen cupboards and returned with a black jar. Tom had to hold Jack down—he said he was getting used to it—as Agnes enlarged the shaven area around the cut with his safety razor which he had fetched from upstairs. She scraped away until she'd bared a piece of skin about three inches square and covered the wound with a piece of clean lint. Over the lint she pressed down a piece of very adhesive Elastoplast and opened her jar. Using a small, blunt knife she carefully 'buttered' the plaster with the contents of the jar, a thick treacly substance and when she'd finished, she patted Jack's head and apparently forgot him while she prepared breakfast.

Left to himself in his corner as the bacon began to sizzle and Tom shouted the first of his ritual calls for Philip and Marjorie to get up, Jack took a quick look at his leg. It was still stiff when he moved it and as the bandage was no longer there it must be the dressing Agnes had put on that was the cause of the trouble. But now he knew it was wrong to pull dressings off, he took stock of the situation before making an attempt. Agnes was occupied at the stove and Tom had gone upstairs to shave. It would be safe to have a quick tug and one good pull should be enough for such a small thing. After all, had he not removed a great deal of the white stuff which had clung to his leg with a grip like an otter? Slyly he moved his head along his flank and sniffed at the black compound covering the plaster. It didn't smell too appetising but that couldn't be helped and after a last look to check that Agnes was engrossed in her cooking, he felt for the edge of the plaster with his tongue. He whipped his head away and put his muzzle into his drinking bowl. His tongue was coated with the most awful tasting mess imaginable. He lapped furiously, trying to rid his mouth of the foul taste and over his slurping he heard Agnes laughing and calling up to Tom.

'He's tried it. Come and have a look at him trying to get rid of it,' she walked across to Jack. 'Now then, lad, let that be a lesson and behave yourself in future.'

The children hurried down with their father, asking what was wrong.

Agnes wagged her finger. 'Remember when you wouldn't stop biting your nails and the stuff I put on them? Well, Jack's got some on his sticking plaster.'

Marjorie was outraged with her mother. 'You haven't, Mum?'

'Yes I have. Now you two go up and get washed and dressed or I'll put some on your bacon.'

The children went, expressing their sympathy for Jack and disgust with her in the same breath.

But Agnes's trick worked and when Jack went back to the vet to have the stitches removed the plaster was still intact and Arthur said he would have taken his cap off to Agnes if he'd been wearing one.

Jack was completely fit again a week later and Tom only had three weeks to get him back into the swing of obedience training so he stepped up the programme to three sessions a day. The only reason he wanted Arthur Cawthorne's five pounds was for the laugh he would get when his friend paid up, but to win a novice event with a dog only just over the six months age minimum would be a real feather in his cap in the dog world.

Jack, of course, didn't know that any special morning had arrived when Tom and Agnes were up an hour earlier than normal but he caught the infectious excitement of the children as Philip held him steady for Marjorie to brush his lengthening coat. At six and a half months he was beginning to take on an adult look and was already as big as many full-grown dogs of his breed. His 'cravat', the white patch in his chest and throat, was the only part of his coat that wasn't jet black and as Ned White commented each time he saw him, he was growing into a damn' fine lookin' animal.

Jack was all about the kitchen watching Tom make sandwiches and fill flasks with tea and coffee as Agnes cooked breakfast but Rex lay bored and disinterested in his corner. He'd seen it all before—the early rising and hurried, excited departure with all the family in the Land Rover, the long, wearisome drive to some strange and distant part, the huge gathering of people with dogs. A year or two ago he would have been as keen as Jack to set off but now he had seen thirteen summers, there was nothing left that could be new to him. He yawned, laid his chin on his paws, closed his eyes and dozed; an old, old man.

Finally the Land Rover was loaded up with food, gumboots, warm coats and Jack, and they were bumping their way along the track out on to the main road. Rex had been left out in the yard, where there was plenty of water for him, to guard the fort against any opportunist who might think it would be a good time to steal a chicken or two.

They went down into the lower country with its fields of grazing cattle, wheat and oat crops and on beyond Jack's birthplace—which he didn't recognise as they passed—through a great area of orchards where the road was closed in with tall hedges which made travelling uninteresting and tiring. After the fruit trees there were more and more buildings until all the world was made of brick, a world noisy with motor cars, large goods vehicles and loud people. And the further they drove into this land of stone and concrete and glass, the louder were the disturbing reverberations of engines and the calling of the people who hurried about the streets. The frightening crescendo came when they were in the largest open space Jack had seen since they'd entered the city, not a *real* open space of grass or moorland, just a place devoid of buildings although it was hemmed in all around with great piles of brick with many windows looking down like sightless eyes. Here there were cars on either side of the Land Rover, and to the front and rear as far as Jack could see, all crawling and jostling in a circle which had a figure of a man as its axis, a man made of stone.

In this place the air was tainted with stinking fumes that were sharp to delicate nostrils and bitterly acrid to a mouth that only knew the pure air of the hill country. Neither two ravenous foxes nor one desperate otter had frightened Jack but he was frightened of the city. He lay on the floor in the back of the Land Rover with his head on his paws listening to the cacophony and breathing the poisonous air. The children who came rarely to 'civilisation' were too agog with everything to bother with Jack and Jack was so cowed he didn't even feel lonely.

That the noise would eventually stop didn't occur to him, he was concerned only with the present, the din and smells that went on and on without respite, assaulting his nose, ears and mouth as though it wanted to put an end to him and when the Land Rover turned off the roundabout, the change in his temporary environment was so slight it didn't register. All the way out of the other side of the city he lay there not moving, until suddenly, it seemed to him, they were out of that mad place and driving through fields again. Green fields with just the rushing wind, hum of the engine and rumble of tyres to listen to. He sprang to his feet, braced himself against the swaying floor and barked for sheer joy at an inoffensive tree.

There was a silence in the car, then the children shouted simultaneously, 'Jack's barked, Dad!'

Tom looked at them through the rear view mirror. 'Nearly all dogs do sooner or later, you know, just like kids talking.'

His lack of enthusiasm for Jack's magnificent achievement only earned their scorn. Philip said defensively, 'That was a smashin' bark for his first time.'

Tom smiled dryly and Agnes turned in her seat, holding out her hand to be licked. Jack craned his neck forward to oblige but was disappointed to find the hand didn't conceal a chocolate drop and went quickly back to watching the passing scenery. He gave voice to an old Retriever waddling along the roadside path with an even older man; then at an Alsatian sitting in the back of a car they were overtaking. He barked at trees, people, lorries, everything and anything, his voice perceptibly strengthening with practice until Tom yelled, *'Quiet! Get down!* You're worse than a bloody woman,' and got Agnes's elbow in his ribs for making the comparison.

Presently the traffic thickened up, mostly with cars and small vans carrying one or more dogs and their speed dropped as they came up to another built-up area, one much more quiet and agreeable than the city. It, too, had an open space around which the cars had to go but the buildings that hemmed in this square were not gigantic monstrosities. They were rows of two-storey shops and houses and instead of the statue in the centre, there were stalls with colourful canvas awnings and under the awnings piles of merchandise with men offering their goods to the shoppers.

It didn't take long to pass through the market town but the Land Rover's progress was still slow when they reached the fields again. Tom kept to the nearside in a crawling queue which, far ahead, was turning left into a country lane.

'Are we nearly there yet?' Marjorie asked.

Tom nodded. 'A mile down that lane up there and you can stretch your legs.'

'I'm hungry,' Philip informed his mother.

'You're never anything else.'

'I bet Jack's hungry as well,' he persisted, hoping rations would be shared out there and then.

'*He's* never anything else, either, but you can just wait till we get there so's we can eat in comfort.'

'And,' Tom added heavily, 'Jack get's nothing to eat till he's been in the ring. Hungry dogs are livelier than full 'uns and I want him obeying the commands this afternoon, not tomorrow morning.'

'Poor Jack,' Marjorie sympathised, 'can't he just have ...'

'No,' Tom mimicked, 'he can't just have a bit of yours and let that be the end of it or you'll stop at home the next time we come to a show.'

Marjorie scrunched down in her seat to pull a face at him and the object of the discussion joined in a barking match with a Yorkshire Terrier in the car behind, filling the Land Rover with an appalling din.

Tom opened his window resignedly. 'Kids, women and dogs. I just can't win.'

The large field adjacent to the one being used as a show ground was already more than half full of cars and vans parked in symmetrical lines by the attendants and on either side of the cars still entering the gate, streams of people and dogs passed on their way to check in. It was noisy here, but not noisy like the city. Cheerfully shouted greetings and the rapturous yelping of excited pups are not frightening and Jack caught the infection of gaiety, darting from one window to another to join in the chorus. The children were anxious to get out amongst it all, stiff and bored after the four-hour drive.

'Look at that Great Dane, Mam.'
'What's that black one, Dad?'
'A Rottweiler.'
'There's another over there.'
'No, that's a Dobermann.'

Tom patiently put up with it, driving into position at the rear of the field on the instructions of the beckoning attendant. He set the handbrake thankfully. 'Right. Hop out. Philip, put Jack's lead on and take him over to the hedge and *don't* go wandering off. Bring him straight back and we'll go get our number.'

As soon as his paws touched the grass all Jack's training and thoughts of obedience flew temporarily out of his head. He strained against the lead to get up close to a Standard Poodle, dragging Philip helplessly in his wake.

Tom bawled, 'What the hell are you playing at, lad? Get him under control!'

'I ca-a-a-n't,' Philip wailed, both arms outstretched as he clung to the lead and hared after his bounding charge. One sniff at the Poodle was enough and Jack took off again, luckily in the direction of the hedge. There he rooted about in the bottom of the hawthorns until he found a suitable place to relieve himself. Then they were off along the hedge bottom, which was very interesting with the scattered scents of hedgehog, mouse and mole. He paused at intervals to raise a leg, nonchalantly ignoring Philip's pleas.

'Jack, *Heel. Heel* Jack. *Stay, Sit, Down.*'

Tom caught up with them at one of the watering points, silently taking the lead from Philip's thankful hand. Jack's next forward rush carried him exactly four feet, to the extent of the lead. With Tom holding the free end of the leather Jack stopped as quickly as if he'd run into a solid wall, reared up and fell over backwards on to his side.

'Heel!' Tom said giving the lead a sharp, hard tug. Jack ran round Tom's right side to sit at his left leg.

'That's the way to do it, lad,' he said to himself. Philip was already halfway back to the sandwiches and orangeade.

'Now then, Tom.' A short, fat man walked across from his car to shake hands and have a look at Jack. 'It's been a long time. Thought you'd finished with showing.'

Tom grinned ruefully. 'I have. I've come for the obedience, believe it or not.'

The fat man ran his experienced eye over Jack. 'He looks all right for a young 'un. Good workin' dogs, them Belgians.'

'Oh, he can do his stuff good enough for Novice but he's never been in a crowd before, he might not settle down in time.'

'Novice?' the fat man raised his eyebrows. 'You might have done better to give him a run with the Beginners for his first time.'

Tom shook his head. 'He's nearly up to Test "B" standard. He'll do all right with the Novices if I can calm him down. I'd better go have a sandwich and see the

Secretary. Meet you in the beer tent about two, we can have a chat there.'

The fat man nodded and went to get his two young Afghan Hounds from his car. These were show dogs, not trained for odedience and like all their breed, ultra playful. Jack whined to join in the romp but Tom said, 'Heel!' firmly and marched him back to the Land Rover.

'We'll give you a run in the exercise area in a bit and then see if we can get you settled down.'

There was a carnival atmosphere in the showground, which was so big it took up two entire fields. In the centre were the show rings, twenty-two in number, in which nearly eighty breeds of dogs, each breed divided into several classes, would be put through their paces and judged for beauty; the winners enhancing their pedigrees. There were also the obedience dogs which would not be judged for beauty at all but purely on the performance of the way they obeyed their handler's commands and these included many off-beat breeds which had no Kennel Club standards and not a few crossbreds and mongrels.

Surrounding the rings were twelve marquees, mostly to provide cover and quarters for the show dogs waiting their turn for judging. One of them housed the equipment of the local catering firm and another, the largest, a tent big enough to hold a three-ring circus, was serving as a bar. In the spaces between the marquees, vendors of every requirement for the canine world had set up smaller tents for the sale of their products, all the famous tinned and packaged foods, leads, collars and jackets, instruments for grooming from claw clippers to trimming shears. One small booth was stocked with all the patent medicines for curing every disease a dog can contract and the sign outside another claimed the occupant to be the most renowned animal photographer in the world. Every available nook and cranny was taken up by hot-dog stalls, ice-cream vans, fish and chip wagons and candy floss machines.

The officials' tent was at the opposite end from the entrance, at the end of the double row of rings, and Tom led the way with Jack through the thickening multitude, with Agnes towing the gaping, overawed children.

'Mam, can I have a hot-dog?'

'I want some candy floss.'

'You've both just eaten goodness knows how many sandwiches, you can wait a bit. You'll make yourselves sick.'

'We won't, aw, go on, Mam.'

'I said no. Now shut up. We'll be losing your father. Come *on*, Marjorie.'

Tom really had his hands full with Jack who was intoxicated with the heady atmosphere and wafted odours of frying onions, sausages and the strong smell as they passed the fish and chip wagons. When Tom snatched him back to heel he'd only remember the command for a matter of seconds and then some new wonder would appear before him to break his concentration and he'd try to dart away again. All the time Tom spoke softly, trying to calm him into a fit state to take commands in case they were amongst the first few to go in the ring. He didn't despair, not quite.

He came from the cool sanity of the officials' tent with a white card bearing '23' pinned to his lapel and found his offspring devouring hot-dogs as though they hadn't eaten for a week, under Agnes's watchful eye.

She asked, 'When are you on?'

'We're twenty-third. There's fifty-eight entries.'

'What a pity, just two short.'

'Why is it a pity?' Philip's question came out, filtered through a partly chewed hot-dog.

Tom explained, 'Because if there's sixty entries or more the whole class is divided in two, dogs and bitches are judged separately so we wouldn't have had as much competition.'

Philip swallowed his mouthful with a gulp. 'Doesn't matter, you're still goin' to win, aren't you, Jack?'

He crouched down to stroke Jack who thought he was offering the last of his hot-dog. He accepted, picking the morsel neatly from Philip's hand and swallowing it without chewing at all, on the offchance that Philip would want it back.

'Hey!' Philip got up. 'Your dog's just pinched my hot-dog,' he told Tom in an aggrieved tone, 'and I'm still hungry.' Tom looked heavenward, defeated, and flipped a fifty-pence piece to his son.

'That's to share—twenty-five pence each, mind,—go get lost for an hour or so but be back here at,' he looked at his watch, 'dead on half past two.'

Philip vanished into the crowd with the speed of a genie with Marjorie hot on his tail, yelling for him to change the coin and hand over her half.

Agnes laughed. 'Come on, let's go have a drink and a sit down while we've got the chance.'

Tom knocked out his pipe on the log he was using as a seat in the field designated as the exercise area. This was the only place in the show that dogs were allowed off the leash, except when they were in the ring It was quarter past two and Jack had been getting rid of his surplus energy by charging about the field with a group of older dogs. Tom hoped he'd be sufficiently worn out to go through the exercises without being distracted by his surroundings. Tom stood up and whistled. Jack's head popped up from the mêlée of the mock fight and then Tom shouted, 'Come, Jack,' and sighed inwardly with relief when the dog ran to him at once, panting, and at a speed noticeably slower than his usual gallop. If the timing was right, Jack wouldn't regain his wind and energy until they'd been in the ring and if that happened, as Tom had planned, they were in with a good chance.

When Tom got to the ring entrance, Agnes had rounded up the children and was waiting for him. 'Number twenty's in now, so it won't be long. They're doing the sits and downs and sixes so there'll only be one after you and then you'll be finished.'

Tom watched numbers twenty-one and twenty-two critically, not seeing anything exceptional about them and walked in with Jack full of confidence. In the ring with them was the judge with his score sheet and the steward who would give Tom the commands to relay to Jack. Tom knew them both—everyone seems to know everyone else in the dog world—and after they'd exchanged a few words the steward led him to the starting point.

The judge said, 'You know the rules, Tom, once we start an exercise you can encourage your dog as much as you like as long as you don't touch him. All right?'

Tom nodded and they were ready.

At this time in the afternoon every aspect at the show was in full swing with stewards in the nearby rings constantly shouting orders to the handlers and children and dogs outside the rings laughing and barking. From time to time announcements were made over a booming public address system and Jack would never be exposed to more unaccustomed distraction than he was then.

'Ready?' asked the steward.

'Ready,' Tom grunted. Jack was sitting by his left leg in the 'Heel' position. The judge nodded at the steward who wasted no more time.

'Handler and dog, forward!'

'Heel!' Tom said sharply, to get Jack's full attention, and stepped off with his left foot. The spectators round the Novice ring quietened as the exercise started although there was still plenty of loud background noise but Jack was there, exactly where he should have been, walking close to Tom's leg, looking up at his master, waiting for the next command. They had nearly reached the other side of the ring before the steward called, 'Right turn!'

Tom said 'Heel' and pivoted, Jack stayed with him, the lead hanging slackly in a curve from Tom's hand to Jack's neck.

'*Halt!*'

Tom slapped his right foot down hard, drew his left one up to it and Jack sat, perfect position again, absolutely square.

'Handler and dog, forward!'

'Heel!' and they were off again at the brisk 'normal' speed which is a little faster than a military march. They went through the gamut, 'Halt', 'Forward', 'About turn', 'Halt', 'Forward', 'Left turn', 'Halt', 'Forward', 'About turn', back to the starting point, and then, 'Finish'.

Jack was allowed to relax for a few seconds at the end of the first exercise and Tom playfully slapped him and told him what a good dog he'd been until the steward asked, 'Ready?'

The second exercise was exactly the same as the first with the exception that it was off the lead, the crucial test for a young dog, but as Tom had hoped, Jack performed beautifully again. Only once did he sit slightly crooked and anyone can be forgiven one mistake. After that there was another moment or two of respite before the 'Recall'.

They went to the same starting point where Tom again carried out the steward's instructions.

'Ready?'

'Ready!'

'Last command to your dog!'

'*Stay!*' Tom said loudly and severely.

'Leave your dog. Forward!'

Tom strode away across the ring trying to will Jack to sit still and not follow him, knowing that dogs, like people, can be adversely affected by important occasions.

'Halt!' A brief pause, then, 'About turn.'

When Tom faced about, Jack was still sitting where he'd left him but he was leaning forward with his neck stretched out, wanting to follow and he almost over-balanced. His hind-quarters didn't move but he had to put his left fore-paw out to save himself from toppling over. After what seemed an interminable pause the steward said, 'Call your dog.'

'*Come, Jack!*'

Jack came eagerly. For a moment Tom thought he was going to arrive too quickly and crash into his legs, which would have cost points, but he slowed down in time and came to a stop precisely where he should have been, sitting facing Tom and looking up for the next command.

'Heel your dog!'

'Heel, Jack!'

Jack moved round Tom's right side, brushing his trousers all the way and a Cruft's champion couldn't have sat more perfectly. For a few seconds the steward made them hold the position, then he smiled and said, 'Finish.'

Tom threw his arms up, 'Good boy, good lad, you'll do for me, Jack.'

Jack bounded about all round his legs and jumped up to touch his chest with his paws showing his pleasure at the praise. The judge came over with his sheet.

'I'm knocking you half a mark off for the crooked sit and half for the recall.'

Tom rubbed Jack's ears, 'We're in with a chance, then?'

The judge inclined his head in agreement. 'Get your dumb-bell for the retrieve, please.'

Tom collected the wooden dumb-bell, the regulation

article to be retrieved by Novices, from Agnes and went back to the starting point. When he had Jack sitting properly at his side the steward asked, 'Ready?'

'Aye.'

'Throw your dumb-bell.'

Tom used the stern tone that had never to be disobeyed, *'Stay!'* and tossed the dumb-bell under-arm across the ring.

The steward's eyes never left Jack and after a pause, 'Send him after it.'

Tom snapped, 'Fetch, Jack!'

Jack hared away, did a skidding turn, snatched up the dumb-bell and charged back. Tom cringed and braced his legs as Jack thudded into them, but having used Tom as a buffer he then sat as required with the dumb-bell in his mouth, eyes glued to Tom's. At the steward's order Tom took the dumb-bell and called Jack to heel. Jack scurried round him over zealously and finished up sitting slightly skew-whiff. They lost another two half marks on that exercise but were still in a strong position, having only dropped an average of half a mark on each exercise.

'When do you want us back?' Tom asked the judge.

'Ten minutes for the next dog and five minutes for me to have a smoke; a quarter of an hour.'

Tom left the ring hurriedly, saying to Agnes as he passed, 'I'll have to go run him again, he's getting a bit too frisky.'

Philip and Marjorie went with him and he used them to keep Jack moving, first one calling him and then the other, so when they returned to the ring the dog was suitably breathless and quite ready for a rest.

The judge lined up six competitors with their dogs along one side of the ring, three Alsatians, a Collie, a black Labrador and Jack. The handlers spent the last few minutes talking softly to the dogs, calming them, giving them confidence until the judge called, 'Prepare to leave your dogs!'

The handlers stood in position to the right of the dogs.

'Last command to your dogs!'

'*Stay!*' Tom ordered along with the others.

'Leave your dogs!'

The handlers, four men and two women, marched away across the ring.

'Halt! Turn to face your dogs! *Time!*'

The steward started the stop watch to tick off the minute the dogs had to remain in position. It was a nerve-wracking minute for the handlers, make or break for those like Tom who were leading the fields on points. Normally, sixty seconds as a period of time is insignificant, but to a young, partly trained dog in the midst of a busy, crowded showground it can be an eternity to be separated from its master.

'Time please?' asked the judge, of the steward.

'Thirty-five seconds.'

Just over the halfway point and the Collie broke, trotting across to its mistress, knowing it was doing wrong, head down in a guilty slink and five seconds later the youngest of the Alsatians followed it. Simultaneously Tom was praying and willing Jack to stay and he stayed, with the other three, until the steward called 'Time' and the judge said, 'Return to your dogs.'

A brief break for praising the dogs and then the judge called them back into line for the 'Down' stay, when the dogs had to lie still with the master across the ring for two minutes. All six came through this with flying colours and immediately they were out of the ring Jack got his reward, a handful of chocolate drops. Tom was making the connection in Jack's mind of the show ring with good things to eat for his future fortification.

'Have we won?' the children wanted to know as Jack

gobbled the chocolate from Tom's palm.

'We won't know that till the end of the show, there's a lot of dogs to go yet, but we got full marks for the stays so we're on ninety-eight per cent. We've a hell of a chance.'

'Good,' said Philip and turned the conversation to more pressing matters. 'Can we have our tea? I'm starving.'

Tom forked out another fifty pence piece. 'You two go get something yourselves and then come to the beer tent. *I* want a drink and I don't suppose I'll have to force one down your mother.'

He didn't. The last dogs wouldn't be judged until about six o'clock and it was going to be a long, long wait.

Chapter 5

(5)

It was almost midnight when the victorious Ewings climbed wearily from the Land Rover and released the hero who ran off for a much needed spate of leg raising. The winner of the Novice Competition had been announced on the P.A.S., 'Mr Tom Ewing with Jacques de Montpelier, ninety-eight per cent,' at a quarter to seven and Tom had collected the rosette and certificate, refusing celebratory drinks from delighted friends on account of the long drive ahead of him. The prize money had been five pounds and there was every prospect that Tom would recover the money he'd paid the breeder for Jack and go on to show a handsome profit, providing Jack lived up to the promise he'd shown. He was initiated into another ritual on the next evening.

On two evenings each week Tom always called Rex and took him away in the Land Rover until it was after the time the dogs were usually asleep, and when they came back they carried with them a scent that was foreign to any Jack had experienced. They carried this smell on their breath and Jack knew it had something to do with the way old Rex flopped down in his corner and went fast asleep with even more speed than he normally did, and the way Tom would laugh a great deal and make a fuss of him, Jack, and Agnes. Sometimes Tom would laugh and tickle Agnes too much and she would snap at him in the sharp reproving tone that must always be obeyed and then Tom would go to bed, walking in an unsteady fashion.

Jack had settled down in his corner, expecting to be left out again, but bounced up, tail swinging like an inverted pendulum, when Tom took his lead from the hook on the wall and called him to the door.

'Tom Ewing,' Agnes said severely as Tom clipped the lead to Jack's collar, 'haven't we got enough with you and that old boozer without teaching a pup bad habits?'

Tom laughed as he opened the door. 'Got to start teaching him to play dominoes some time. Old Rex starts getting spots before his eyes now when he's had a couple of pints.'

Agnes snorted her disgust.

They went off the estate into the village and parked outside a smallish building with brightly lighted windows and the sound of loud voices coming from the swing doors.

Rex, of course, as befits a tried and trusted dog, was not on the lead and he trotted up to push the doors open with his muzzle and nip quickly inside before the doors could swing back to trap his tail. Jack went uncertainly with Tom into the smoky atmosphere. The place was fairly full of men, mostly sitting around tables or leaning on the long wooden counter and Jack knew it was feeding time here because everyone was drinking from glasses and many were eating potato crisps from paper bags. Jack knew what crisps were as sometimes Philip or Marjorie would slip him one when Tom wasn't there.

Ned White was in a deep conversation at the corner of the bar with the vet and Tom walked up, grinning and holding out his hand. Arthur looked down at Jack with disapproval as he handed a five-pound note to Tom.

'You've cost me money, you little bugger. Still, I suppose you deserve a drink for winning. Where's Rex?'

'Where do you think?' Tom asked, pointing to a corner.

There sat Rex, close up to a drinking bowl of the same type they used at home, mouth open, tongue lolling, a picture of eager expectancy.

'Two halves o' mild,' Arthur said to the man behind the bar and the saliva drooled from Rex's mouth as the beer was poured into the bowl. At a click of Tom's fingers the old dog dropped his head to lap greedily and noisily and continuously until every bead of moisture had been scooped out by his practised tongue. He sat watching with the same rapturous expression as Arthur poured in the second half pint and slunk unwillingly to heel, as though he had been cheated, when Tom called him.

Arthur took Jack's lead and led him to the bowl. Jack sniffed the brown liquid carefully and tested the thick, close bubbles with the tip of his tongue. Not quite sure whether he liked it he made two quick laps, cutting through the foam into the liquid, licked his lips and drew back. Arthur shook his head slowly, handing Jack back to Tom.

'Told you he was a wrong 'un. You can never trust a teetotaller.'

Tom rubbed Jack's ears. 'He's only a lad, he'll learn. Go on, Rex, see it off.'

Rex had never to be given any command twice but this one he obeyed before Tom had finished speaking and in no time at all the bowl was wiped clean again and Rex was sitting smartly to attention hoping for another delivery. He never moved from that spot all evening and his vigil was rewarded with another two glasses of beer. Jack was put down in a corner with a bag of crisps as a substitute, for which he was grateful.

When the crisps had been disposed of, and with no more forthcoming, Jack lost interest in the taproom of the Bull and had a long, boring wait, continually having to be put back in the corner from where he kept emerging to nudge Tom's leg in a plea to be taken outside. Finally the man behind the bar, who Jack understandably mistook for a show ring judge, shouted 'Time!' and shortly after that they were back in the Land Rover on the way home. Jack sat next to Tom on the front passenger seat while Rex settled himself on the rear bench seat and went to sleep.

Agnes seemed to be waiting for them with foot-tapping impatience and as Tom closed the door he went straight into the attack, that being the best form of defence.

'Now before you start, do you think I'd give a young dog like him any beer? All he had was a packet of crisps. Honest.'

Agnes's expression plainly said she didn't fully believe him but, woman-like, she sniffed and tossed her head at the recumbent Rex.

'Well it looks as though he's had enough for both of them. I ought to report you to the R.S.P.C.A.'

'What's good for a man's good for a dog, love.'

'Good?' his wife said. 'Good? And I remember you telling the kids they hadn't to teach him any bad habits!'

Tom knew the futility of trying to argue logically with a woman. He contented himself by making a large beef sandwich for his supper.

As Christmas approached, Jack was taught to retrieve game and this was a vastly different proposition to retrieving a tasteless dumb-bell. It took Tom hours of patient schooling to get him to let go of a warm, freshly killed animal pervaded with the taste of hot blood. But just in time for the pheasant shoot, Tom succeeded. They went out into a thick December frost to pick up Ira Love and thin out the first of the copses.

The morning was clear and bright with a strong sun that couldn't be looked into for long, windless and calm, just about perfect shooting conditions. The crisp nip of the new winter even put a little giddy life into Rex and he ran in the clear tracks of Jack's aimless bounding.

'Where do you want to start?' Tom asked the expert.

'In them bottom trees near the river'll be best. There'll be a brace or two in them bushes.'

They started at the southern end of the stand of trees, the men about fifty yards apart, the two old dogs, Rex and Dapper foraging in front to flush out the birds and Jack, as always, at Tom's heel. They expected good sport as the standard of marksmanship of the year's visitors had been anything but good.

Dapper moved in a fast zig-zag, nose to the ground, quartering the small areas of open grass amongst the bushes, Ira shouting encouragement non-stop.

'Seek, Dapper, find 'em, that's a good lad.'

Rex's method was to go directly to a bush or patch of tall grass and stick his head in, growling horribly. Jack whined constantly to be released to join in the fun. Overhead startled birds, mostly pigeons, flapped up to circle and reconnoitre the cause of the disturbance. When Dapper's tail went up, Ira snapped his gun to his shoulder. As the dog tracked into the stiff undergrowth the first pheasant, a long tailed cock, skimmed the ground briefly and started to rise through the trees at a forty-five degree angle. Ira swung his gun smoothly, firing when the pheasant was twenty feet from the ground and from controlled, beautiful flight the corpse curved limply down, wings still spread, to hit the base of a tree with a heavy thud. Dapper ran to retrieve the bird unbidden and Ira dropped it into his bag, sending the dog away again.

The boom of the shotgun acted like a starter's pistol. From three other places, terrified pheasants rose with noisy wings whirring and Tom brought one down with his first cartridge but shot too hastily with his second, a hen bird speeding quickly out of range. Ira was successful with his second try and as Dapper went to retrieve again,

Tom dropped Rex flat and sent Jack to bring in his first kill.

'Fetch it!'

Jack tore across the brittle grass like a greyhound, his breath a white, dispersing streamer in the cold air. He skidded to an ungainly stop, snatched up the pheasant and raced back to Tom.

'Good lad,' Tom said, holding out his hand. With the bird hanging from his mouth, Jack retreated a pace.

'Come on, that's a good boy,' Tom coaxed, reaching out. Jack walked back another yard.

'Down!' Tom commanded. Jack dropped flat still holding on to the pheasant and Tom had to force his jaws open to get the prize. As soon as the bird was out of sight, in the bag slung from Tom's shoulder, Jack ran round Tom to sit at heel, mouth open, tongue hanging. Tom tapped him on the head with a forefinger.

'Never mind sitting there grinning. You let go of 'em first time. *Heel*.' He hurried to catch up with Ira, sending on Rex to join Dapper in the foraging.

Birds fell regularly to the guns throughout the day and when they went back to the Land Rover in the dusk, both bags were crammed and both men had birds, tied together in pairs, slung across their arms and shoulders. The money they would bring from the clamouring hotels would be a good boost for the estate finances.

They stopped for a drink at Ira's cottage, milk for the dogs and beer for the men, then set off home with the birds piled in the back of the Land Rover, two very weary dogs and one highly satisfied man.

A haloed, slim crescent of a moon painted the countryside with a silver tint, giving the earth an ethereal quality of far distances that were not there. A small hillock a few hundred yards away looked like a mountain on the horizon of a vast plain until the swaying, rolling, white headlights brought it into perspective. Tom smoked his pipe and hummed, Rex snored gently on the rear seat and Jack sat beside Tom quietly watching the passing scene; for once he had had the energy really burned out of him by sheer hard work.

The hillock was a massive rabbit warren but even the flash of white scuts, as the rabbits bolted to safety in the glare of the headlights, failed to arouse any interest in Jack. He'd had his fill of game and retrieving and running, and the rabbits would still be there tomorrow if Tom decided to thin out that colony.

When Jack saw the strange dog, though, he did snap to attention, sitting bolt upright, ears pricked, and as the Land Rover moved on, he turned on the seat to see the dog disappear behind the hill again. Tom sensed more than saw that something had disturbed him and although it might have been nothing of importance he had to get through to Jack in his formative days that vigilance was essential on the estate and that any warnings he gave would be investigated and rewarded. He drove on until a bend in the track and a stand of trees hid the Land Rover from the hillock and there he parked, letting two suddenly very lively dogs out into the clear night.

'Down!' he said softly as he gently closed the door. He reloaded the gun, tucked it under his arm, broken, pointed Rex back in the direction they had come and whispered, 'Seek, Rex, seek!'

He kept hold of Jack's collar as the old dog ran silently on the grass beside the track and went out of sight around the bend.

'Heel!' he murmured. He too kept off the hard ground, walking carefully after Rex, Jack once more unwillingly at his side when he wanted to be off in front with Rex.

The peace of the night was shattered by savage growls and barks before they reached the bend and Tom started to run. He knew it wasn't Rex who was barking. Rex didn't bark when he was fighting, he concentrated on disposing of his adversary with maximum speed and minimum effort.

As they neared the hillock the excitement became too much for Jack and he streaked off, a black silent shadow against the silvery grey ground, heedless of Tom's commands to 'Heel'. Recklessly he slewed around the topside of the steep little hump to see Rex with the death-bringing throat-hold on the strange dog and a man swing a heavy stake down sickeningly on to his head. Rex collapsed across the body of his gasping foe who came to life when the grip relaxed and struggled from underneath to get shakily to its feet. Jack barked and the man turned.

'Christ, another! Must be someone with 'em. Come on, Laddo.'

The man dropped his stake and with the rapidly recovering Laddo, a Golden Labrador, close on his heels he ran round the far side of the hillock. Jack could hear Tom coming nearer and was confused about what he should do. When Tom appeared, Jack was sniffing at Rex who was regaining his senses and trying to raise his head. Tom paused for a brief look at the injury, an open scalp wound, and knowing the remarkable recuperative powers of dogs, he snapped, 'Come on, Jack, heel. We'll catch 'em with a bit o' luck.'

Together, man and dog rounded the small hill and started the chase. The quarry was now about a hundred and fifty yards away, across the track, running to the south. A mile away, on the other side of the most southerly part of the estate's streams, the perimeter fence was broken by a cattle grid and from there a service track led to the main road. Ned White hauled his timber out from that area instead of a tortuous journey the length of the property. That would be where the poacher would have parked his vehicle.

Tom Ewing was fitter than most men approaching middle-age but the man in front was obviously many years younger and try as he would, Tom couldn't narrow the gap. He pursued steadily and hopefully over ground which was treacherous and ever ready to snag an unwary foot in the pale, deceiving moonlight, but when they crossed the stream by the rough wooden bridge, the distance seemed to have increased and he knew that if the poacher had a reliable vehicle he was going to escape. Tom had one chance left. An untried, untested chance who was trotting at his side. Tom remembered the way Jack had fearlessly fought with the otter, the speed in those legs which would outrun any Labrador and he took his chance.

'Away, Jack. Fetch 'em,' he panted.

Jack was away at the word 'fetch' without really understanding what was expected of him. He'd seen Rex trying to kill the dog and the man try to kill Rex and he'd grasped the idea that this was a chase but he'd never been taught to dislike his own kind and the only instructions he'd had towards humans was to respect them. There was no way for him to know that some humans are infinitely more cunning and desperate than any wild animal and therefore more dangerous, so he stretched his legs, giving vent to his exuberance with an occasional bark, and swiftly closed the gap.

The running man glanced over his shoulder and cursed, believing he was being caught by an experienced guard dog against which an unarmed man had very little, or even no chance. As he ran, he pulled a heavy clasp knife from his jacket pocket, thumbing open a blade worn short with constant honing, a blade that could gralloch a poached roe buck. He knew the pursuing man could not catch him before he got to his van and if he could deal quickly with the dog his escape was assured. Contrary to popular belief, poachers are not always looked upon with tolerance by kindly magistrates and let off with an insignificant fine. Poachers are criminals in exactly the same sense as any other thieves and those with a long list of previous convictions are equally liable to wind up in prison. This one was well-known to the police and courtrooms of the lower country, hence his expedition to the estate.

Jack ran wide and turned quickly to face the man, blocking his path, going naturally into a half crouch, ready to spring. The instinct, passed down from his ancestors, was taking over. The same instinct which had driven them to do battle with wolves, the urge to protect his master and his property; the main reason for the careful breeding of the Belgian Sheepdog.

The poacher's Labrador was an excellent working dog—or he would have been no use to the poacher—but he was at heart a gentle creature who wished harm to no one, a dog without the least desire to fight and he was still suffering somewhat from the punishment Rex had dished out. The Labrador stood uncertainly, not even offering a growl. The poacher waved his knife and swung a boot at Jack and tried to move round him. Still in the half crouch Jack stayed in front of him with a series of jerky little springs, barking loudly each time he moved.

The sweat ran down the poacher's face as he tried again, desperately, to kick Jack but Jack was always too quick, dodging the boot and even snapping at it. Tom was getting closer.

The poacher said to his dog, 'Fetch him, Laddo, fetch him.'

To Laddo the order to fetch referred strictly to dead game and as there was none of that about he stood where he was, puzzled. Whichever way the poacher moved,

Jack jumped in front of him with a bark and a snap which would have deterred anyone from getting too near those bared teeth. And then it was too late for the poacher. Tom came up, panting:

'All right—put—that—knife—away,' and kept the shotgun pointing at the poacher's middle. 'What's your name?'

'Mickey Mouse.'

'All right Mickey Mouse, you'll be parked down by the cattle grid, your vehicle number'll be as good as your name. Let's go have a look at it. Come on.'

He motioned with the gun for the poacher to move.

The poacher hesitated. 'Look, mate. I was only after a rabbit or two,' he pleaded, *'and* I got none. Me nets are up there near the warren and I 'aven't got a gun. How about if I give you a couple o' quid and ...' Tom shook his head. 'All right, I'll make it a fiver if ...'

Tom was firm. 'No chance! Rabbits today, pheasant, partridge, deer tomorrow. Let's go have a look at your licence plate, I've had a long day. *And,*' he added, 'you might as well tell your mates—if you've got any—that Scargill estate is crawlin' with dogs and you fellers have no chance up here.'

The poacher shrugged. 'Okay, I'm Harry Nelson from over near Tarnside ... but I only wanted a couple o' rabbits, honest ... for the pot. That's all.'

'More likely every rabbit on the estate for some butcher who's not too fussy where his meat comes from. Come on, let's see if you've got anything in your van.'

Harry Nelson walked in front with his dog and Tom followed with Jack.

The old van was where Tom had expected, parked under a tree close to the cattle grid and he looked inside by the light of a match. It was empty and clean as a whistle —just a bit too clean.

'What's your job?' he asked.

Harry Nelson smiled wryly. 'Bit o' this an' a bit o' that.'

'A bit of this you were trying tonight is about all the work you do. You're a professional is my guess and I'll bet this isn't the first time you've been caught. Van scrubbed out clean in case the people who aren't too fussy where the game comes from *might* be fussy about how it's delivered and that sounds as though you've a big hotel or two on your books. No gun or snares which shows you're clever enough not to bring anything incriminating that you don't actually need to use. And this isn't the first time you've been here or you wouldn't have known about that rabbit warren. Well, some butcher's going to be disappointed tomorrow.'

Tom took a note of the vehicle licence number, called Jack and walked away without looking back. What Harry Nelson said quietly to his retreating black silhouette was unprintable.

They met Rex on the wooden bridge. The blood had congealed thickly and covered the top of his skull like a cap and he was walking slowly and wearily. He flopped down on to his belly when he saw them. Jack got to him first to sniff at the gash and Tom struck a match.

'Get out of the way, Jack. Sit!' His voice tailed off, and then, 'The bastard. If I'd had any thoughts about letting Harry Nelson off, he's had it now. I hope he goes to gaol for Christmas. Come on, old lad, let's get you home and looked after.'

Harry Nelson would not have spent Christmas in prison or anywhere else if Agnes Ewing had got her hands on him that night. There were twenty-five brace of dead birds to be hung but she had no time for anything but Rex. She gently washed the wound clean while Tom telephoned for Arthur Cawthorne and then sat on the floor with the old head in her lap. She treated the dog as though he was one of her own children, stroking his muzzle and talking softly all the time. Tom raised his eyebrows and sighed but he didn't say anything. Even when he told, somewhat exaggeratedly, of Jack's part in the capture it did nothing to lessen her rage or curb her impatience for Arthur to hurry up.

When he came, he put five stitches in the cut and told Tom to bring Rex to the surgery for X-rays the next day. He feared a fracture of the skull.

The day ended for Jack with an extra feed of rabbit, a whole pint of milk and a great deal of fuss-making and romping with Philip and Marjorie. He slept that night, the sleep of one who earns his living.

The first job, before it was time to go to the surgery, was to go back to the hillock and pick up the evidence against Harry Nelson. Tom realised that he ought to have done it before. When he saw the poaching equipment he whistled. There were two large rolls of light but strong nylon netting and a canvas bag full of wooden pegs. It was easy to see there was sufficient netting to surround the entire warren—all excepting one hole. It was the old tried and true method of pegging the net to cover every hole but one and fanning smoke down that one which would drive out the rabbits into the net, where he could walk round at his leisure knocking them on the head with the heavy stave he'd used on Rex. There was also a plastic bag of oily rags for the fire and a haversack containing tea and sandwiches. Evidently Harry Nelson was a man who gave thought to his work. As Tom had guessed, a professional.

The X-rays showed a slight depression of the skull that wasn't too serious, much to Agnes's relief who had insisted on going with them, and after the vet's, Tom drove on to the police to make his report.

The village constable, a regular patron of the Bull and

a crony of Tom's, insisted on going out to the Land Rover to have a look at Rex before telephoning his colleague in Tarnside. He looked up at Tom with the receiver still to his ear.

'Oh aye, Tom, they know Harry Nelson all right. They say if last night was his first time on your place you're bloody lucky. They say he can find game where there isn't any and if he'd had enough time there wouldn't have been any on your estate. Seems as though all the farmers are up to his tricks around Tarnside an' he's had to break new ground. A good poacher, if good's the right word, is a bloody menace.'

'No more of a menace than the people who buy off him. Anyway,' Tom leaned down from his chair to rub Jack's ears, 'this lad sorted him out all right. He won't come back to Scargill in a hurry.'

They drove back to the estate quickly to drop off Agnes and Rex—the vet had said he should take it easy for a day or two—and then went straight on up through the middle of the rough country to where Ned was helping Ira with the pheasant shooting in Tom's absence. With the extra gun they had a bigger bag than the first day and a thoroughly worn out Jack almost had to crawl from the Land Rover into the kitchen that evening, although he did find the strength from somewhere to eat his dinner quickly enough. Rex ate nothing, doing no more than raise his head to lap disinterestedly a couple of times at his milk and lowering his head on to his paws and drifting off to sleep.

Tom watched him carefully as he ate his own meal and said thoughtfully to Agnes, 'I'd better get Jack started with tracking tomorrow.'

His wife glanced from him to the old dog. 'Aye,' she agreed softly.

Chapter 6

(6)

Any dog can follow a scent, so it might be assumed that any dog can track. This is not so. Tracking, as opposed to the random following of any interesting scent, is the channelling of the dog's talents into proper disciplined paths, persuading the dog to stick to the one scent desired by the handler and ignoring all others which may bisect it, however intriguing they may be. When a dog will faithfully stick to the trail of a man which is constantly crossing the paths of foxes, rabbits, deer and every other animal which lives in the wilds, that dog can be called a tracking dog. Tom started to teach Jack the ways of the hunter on the morning after the visit to the vet's.

Rex was still very much under the weather, walking slowly out after breakfast to answer the call of nature and then walking even more slowly back to his corner where he lay down and drank only a small amount of the milk Agnes gave him before putting his head to the floor and lying perfectly motionless with wide, glazed, unseeing eyes. He didn't turn his head when Tom called Jack to take him to work and wasn't in the least bit curious when, for the first time in more than twelve years, he was left at home.

Tom and Jack went to the extreme south-east of the estate to a small, rocky, almost barren area which was of very little value to grazing animals and would therefore hold few distracting scents. Tom left Jack tied to a bush behind a rocky outcrop where he wouldn't be able to see what was going on as the track was laid. This first lesson had to be the very simplest and Tom touched the ground, every yard or so, with a piece of fresh meat and left a very clear trail about fifty yards long starting at the Land Rover. He left the meat at the end, covered with grass to make Jack track all the way until he was on top of it and went to get the pupil.

He put on the tracking harness, an arrangement of leather straps which fitted snugly around Jack's chest and shoulders with a twenty-foot line attached to the back with which Tom could guide him without breaking his concentration.

'Seek, Jack,' Tom said urgently, tapping the ground where he'd first touched it with the meat, 'Seek, seek!' Jack snuffled about until he picked up the delicious scent whereupon he remained glued to the spot, rooting in the sparse grass for the meat that should have been there.

'Seek, seek!'

Tom tugged the line to get him moving along the track but practically had to drag him to the next place. This performance was repeated all the way until they got to the meat and Jack gulped his reward for a successful track.

Back to his bush went Jack as Tom laid the second one and although Tom had again to guide him to each clue, the dog obeyed the tug of the harness more readily. Unlike obedience work which had to be done in small doses so as not to bore the dog, finding food was a game Jack was prepared to play all day and every day and by lunchtime he'd become quite adept at uncovering the pieces of meat and was ready to go on to the next stage, a zig-zag track but still with the meat as an inducement.

At noon when Tom thought they'd done enough for one day, Jack was happily heading in the direction of the bush, prepared to do it all again. Tom called him to heel.

'Oh no, lad, we're off home. I've earned something to eat as well as you.'

They went tracking every day, Tom making the trails more and more difficult to follow but Jack learned how to quarter the ground and to pick up a lost track. At the end of January Tom introduced other items for him to find; an old spark plug, a comb, a button, the reward of meat coming from Tom's pocket after every success.

And two months after the first attempt on the barren ground Tom said to Agnes, 'He's tracking like a good 'un now.' Coming from Tom that was the equivalent of an international diploma.

As Jack's education, physical strength and general zest for life went on, so Rex's vitality declined. He was in a permanent mood of despondency, eating little and not caring whether he was out in his once beloved country, left in the Land Rover or at home sleeping in his corner. His wound had healed perfectly to all intents and purposes but regular treatment from Arthur Cawthorne did nothing to lift his lethargy.

After one regular visit the vet shook his head. 'No good me telling you to come again, Tom, you'd be wasting your money, I've done all I can. You'll just have to put him out to grass and let him potter about in his own way. He's too old, that's the top and bottom of it.'

From that moment Rex went into full retirement and Jack, who had still a great deal to learn about his trade, was promoted to number one working dog at Scargill Croft. Rex didn't seem to mind and even appeared to enjoy curling up at the south side of the house to sleep the afternoon away when the new spring brought the warmth of the sun. His appetite got better but never reached the sharpness of his younger days when he ate his two-pound meat ration and looked for more. He never failed to amble over to the Land Rover to greet the returning workers in the evenings but his eagerness for Tom's attention had waxed and a friendly word and a stroke was enough for him. He was content.

For Jack, the world was opening up. The tracking harness was put away until such time as there would be another young dog to train and the leather lead stayed in the Land Rover, except when they left the estate to go to the village or on a rare shopping expedition to the distant city. He was heeling free now, working solely to Tom's commands without the necessity of a tug on the chain choker to make him buck up his ideas. Along with the tracking, he had learned to follow the directions of Tom's hand signals and as long as they could see each other, Tom could direct him to any given spot. For the occasions when they couldn't see each other, he would answer to Tom's whistles, a high pitched note which carried further than the human voice but which was perfectly clear to canine ears. Rapidly they were becoming a single working unit with Jack the far-ranging extension of Tom's mind.

They were out early one morning with the gun to bag a few rabbits for the pot when, unusually for him, Tom completely missed a fine buck rabbit. On the spur of the moment he snapped, 'Fetch it, Jack.'

They had manoeuvred in between the rabbits and their warren and the buck was making a wide, semi-circular detour round them to get to the safety of his hole. Jack streaked away to cut off the escape, the early morning sun gleaming on his jet black coat, and his bounding paws throwing up the heavy dew in light-catching showers. Tom regretted not having a camera.

When the buck realised he was not going to make it

to safety, he turned east, away from the dog and the man and for a while, on the flat, held his lead. But the flat going didn't last long, it didn't anywhere at Scargill, and soon he was twisting and turning up a rocky slope with patches of gorse and bracken. His speed was cut down by negotiating the obstacles and his hind-legs often slipped as he scrambled upward.

But what are obstacles for a rabbit, are nothing to a grown dog and as soon as they left the flat grass, Jack started to gain. Twist and turn and leap as he might, the buck could hear Jack coming closer and terror gave him strength and agility beyond his normal powers. Had he been born with the cunning of a fox he would have tried to work his way back down the hill to get to his own element, but rabbits are not artful and he kept on going up even though he could hear Jack panting on his tail. The end came when he was faced with an extra large rock that was too high for him to clear. With thick bracken growing to the right, the only way for the rabbit to go was to the left and Jack anticipated the move. As the buck turned, Jack gathered his hind-legs for one mighty leap and then his teeth closed on the neck fur. A twist of the head, a quick jerk up and the lifeless body arched over Jack's back. Faintly, Tom's shout came on the still air.

'Fetch it, Jack.'

Jack picked up the warm, sagging body and carried it, with a suitably triumphal air, to his master.

After the discovery that he was a natural hunter who had instinctively made his first kill cleanly and without savaging the rabbit, there were as many rabbits unbruised by pellets eaten at Scargill Croft as not. Of all the many tasks he performed Jack liked hunting the best.

In the course of his second summer he became a familiar and favourite figure at the showgrounds, moving easily through the progressively harder tests 'A', 'B' and 'C'. The rosettes and certificates for first, second and third place were mounted on the Ewings' sideboard and Tom said it looked as though they had a real champion on their hands.

True to the prediction of his breeder he did grow too big to be a show dog but that was something Tom couldn't have cared less about. He was beautifully proportioned, standing twenty-seven inches high at the withers with a deep, broad chest set off by his snow-white cravat. His collarette of extra long hair was like a mane and his long tail resembled a huge plume. The muscular legs could carry him all day at a steady lope and, when the occasion demanded, could thrust him forward with lightning acceleration. But experience had added craft and eliminated some of his impetuousness. Whereas he would once have charged his prey too soon, he had now learned the value of stalking, of keeping downwind and making his move at the most advantageous moment and very few rabbits eluded his powerful jaws when he'd made up his mind to catch them.

One August morning the family rose earlier than usual and by the amount of bustling about, the making of sandwiches and filling of flasks, Jack knew he was going to another show. He was on the one-meal-a-day of a fully grown dog now although he was still given a pint of milk in the mornings. When he'd drunk his milk the children brushed and groomed him while Tom ate his breakfast. There was no need to hold him now, he stood placidly as the children each took a side of him and argued afterwards about who had done the best job. When the Land Rover was ready, only Tom climbed into it with him, Agnes and the children wishing them luck and waving as they drove away.

It was a very long run, longer than any Jack had ever made before and they drove along the M.1, stopping at midday for Tom to eat his lunch. It was late in the afternoon when they drove into a city so big it was a nightmare to Jack. Everywhere and endlessly the roads were filled with honking, hooting vehicles and Jack lay quiet in Rex's old place on the rear passenger seat, nostrils twitching at the tainted air. It seemed to Jack that they crawled for an eternity through that hell of stench, noise, and even more disturbing vibrations which thrummed into his ears and down the whole length of his body, making him subdued and nervous at the same time. But finally they turned into a narrow street and swung into a car park behind a tall building with many windows. There, the roar of the traffic was muted and he thankfully followed Tom out to stretch mightily, yawn and relieve himself against a tall lamp-post as there were no trees. There wasn't even a blade of grass to be seen.

Tom gave him a few minutes to explore the car park, then put him back in the Land Rover and went into the building. Jack watched anxiously as the door swung shut behind him, sitting bolt upright on the front seat, nose thrust up close to the windscreen. There he stayed, rigid as a statue, and whining occasionally until Tom came back.

They walked through the busy street, Jack on the lead, to a park which was surrounded on all sides with streams of the inevitable traffic, but at least there was grass and some trees and a stretch of water with ducks and swans. Tom slipped the lead to let him run and have a roll and a cooling swim. They stayed an hour in the park and then it was time to go back to the Land Rover where Tom locked him in again with his dinner.

This time Tom was away longer and Jack was asleep when he came back, at dusk, to put the lead on and take him into the streets again. They didn't go to the park but walked a long way in wide, straight thoroughfares where the shop windows were brilliantly lit although the shops were closed for business. They came to another of the open spaces hemmed in by buildings with the perpetually circling traffic and this one had a fountain as well as a statue at its centre. As they threaded in and out of the hurrying people all Jack wanted was to go home, back to the freedom of the open land and away from this foreign place.

Instead they went into a maze of little side streets and entered a building which, although it didn't resemble the Bull at all, Jack could see was the same kind of place. Men and women were leaning on the bar or sitting at tables drinking beer, laughing or arguing.

Tom put Jack down, with a packet of crisps, in the quietest corner and talked to some of the men as he drank his beer. He was sitting next to Jack and kept dropping his hand down to be licked or to rub Jack's ears but no amount of comforting would have set Jack completely at ease in that place and he was immensely relieved when the barman shouted the familiar *'Time'* and they went back out into the streets. There were still a lot of cars about but it was immeasurably quieter and the long walk back to the Land Rover wasn't too bad. Tom opened the door and Jack sprang in expecting to go home now, but Tom stroked his neck.

'Sorry old lad, but they won't let you into the hotel. You'll have to sleep in here. Still, it's only for one night.'

That night was a long one. Jack had never slept anywhere but in the peace of his own corner in the kitchen at home and he sat for hours, watching the hotel door, expecting Tom to come back for him. The sounds of the city had died to a distant whisper before he wearily lay down and slept. He was awakened many times, once by a pair of patrolling policemen who stopped to look in at him and now and again by a throbbing taxi engine delivering a late arrival to the hotel.

He was awake when the first probing fingers of the sun began to lighten the sky and he listened to the steady build-up of the traffic noise until it reached its daytime proportions again. And when it was impossible to sleep he sat watching the door for Tom.

When Tom did come, he brought a bottle of milk which Jack drank greedily, for the pure, clean taste cleared his mouth of the acrid exhaust fumes, and after a short run about the car park Tom put him back in the vehicle. He wagged his tail and nudged Tom happily; they were going home now.

But they went only a short distance through the pandemonium, to another large building, and here cars were forming up in lines and the scene was familiar. It was the same as arriving at a show but there were no fields or tents and the handlers were taking the dogs into the building. Tom put Jack on the lead and joined them.

Inside the building there were the familiar show rings with busy stewards hurrying about, calling names and organising. The handlers were letting the dogs sniff the strange ground to get used to the place.

Like everything else Jack had seen in this city, the inside of the building was enormous, with a great apexed roof which echoed shouted commands and barks, so he was not only surrounded by the noise he so much disliked but also had his sensitive ears bombarded from above. The other dogs there were all more experienced than Jack and perhaps lived in cities for they were perfectly at ease, ready to make friends with any of the others, but Jack stayed close to Tom's left leg.

The interminable wait to go into the ring was longer than ever and Tom took him outside many times to run in the exercise area, syphoning off some of his bursting energy and nervous tension to make sure he would be his obedient self when they went in the ring.

When they went in, it was all right. The people hushed, the odd bark of the dogs being the only distraction and by that time Jack had become accustomed to the Steward's commands bouncing back from the roof. He worked well at heel, and the sendaway when Tom had to drop him flat inside a white lined square at the far side of the ring, and he found the piece of cloth carrying the scent of the judge quite easily although it was lying amongst four decoys. He went through all the exercises, ate his bag of chocolate drops which were his reward for working well and sat back looking up at Tom, ready to go home.

But it wasn't time to go home. They had lost only a few marks and were in with a good chance, so they had to wait until the results were given in the evening. They went out to walk in the streets, partly to pass away the hours and partly to try to get Jack accustomed to the city bustle. And, for Tom, the wait was worthwhile. Jack was declared Champion by one half-mark over the dog which had been most favoured to win and then everybody wanted to look at Jack and pat him and see his rosette.

A tall, thin man with a shaggy, unkempt Border Collie who had come second to Jack nodded at Tom.

'Now then,' he said, looking at Jack from all angles, ''ow much does tha' want for 'im?'

Tom grinned. 'More than you could pay, Charlie.'

'How's tha' know? Give us yer price.'

'Charlie,' Tom said, still smiling, 'there's not enough money in the Bank of England to buy this feller. You're wasting your time.'

Charlie sucked at a back molar. 'Well, if tha' changes thi' mind, tha' knows where ah live.'

Charlie wasn't the only one interested in buying Jack now that he was a celebrity. A plump, soft-spoken man talked to Tom, as his affectionate wife knelt to pet Jack.

'Excuse me, is your dog for sale?'

Tom shook his head, 'No, thanks.'

The woman was smoothing Jack's woolly-textured cravat.

'Say, you're a real honey, wouldn't *I* just love to own *you*.'

The plump man smiled indulgently over the top of his wife's head. 'Mr Ewing, I believe every man has his price and I'm willing—and able—to pay more than most for anything my wife wants, so let's get down to it. How much? And he's going to a good home, he'll live on a ranch with ...'

'No, there's no ...' Tom cut in on the American but the American came straight back.

'Let me finish, Mr Ewing. I'm Karl Landseer, Rock Springs, Montana, and my ranch there is damn near as big as England. I've been an animal man all my life an' your dog would be joining the best company. My wife buys champion dogs like most women buy nylon stockings, I guess she's hooked on 'em. But are they looked after! Two full-time kennel maids and if some of the people in India and Africa saw what those dogs get to eat, well, I'm telling you there *would* be a revolution.'

He stopped to nod down at his wife and at the way she was lovingly making friends with Jack, as if to give proof of his argument.

Tom took the opportunity to get a word in. 'Mr Landseer, I just had an enquiry from one of the most famous handlers in this country and I told him there isn't enough money in the Bank of England to buy Jack. If I tell you there isn't enough gold in Fort Knox, perhaps you'll begin to understand. You see he's not just an obedience champion, he's a down-to-earth working dog, he does a job every day and I couldn't manage my estate without him.

And he's more than that. To my wife and kids he's every bit as much a pet as your wife would like to make him.'

Karl Landseer studied Tom for a moment and shrugged.

'Honey, Mr Ewing means it.' His wife gave Jack a final pat and stood up. 'Well, I can't say I blame you—but if you ever change your mind, Mr Ewing, write to us care of General Delivery, Rock Springs, Montana.'

Karl Landseer shook Tom's hand and drifted away with his wife to look at some Collies. Tom had meant every word he said about not selling Jack. He was not a rich man, but comfortable, well able to live in the only style he desired and, considering himself happy, he had no yearning for a fat bank balance. But he wouldn't have been human if he hadn't been flattered because what amounted to an almost open cheque offer for Jack was a reflection on his ability as a handler as much as anything else. He looked down at open-mouthed, tongue-lolling Jack and grinned.

'You're a good lad, everybody's after you. Come on, let's go for a walk.'

It was too late to start the drive home that evening and as he was a man who liked a drink, and as he'd as much to celebrate as any dog handler ever had, he went back to the pub he'd been in the evening before. This time he wasn't a complete stranger and when he'd settled Jack down in the corner he was drawn immediately into a conversation with four football fans. Inevitably the talk drifted to other sports and pastimes and Tom couldn't resist telling them about Jack. Like sporting men everywhere they were delighted to be in the presence of a champion and beer flowed Tom's way like water, his acquaintances refusing to let him pay.

Jack came in for a great deal of attention with someone going over to stroke and talk to him every few minutes. For once, understandably, Tom relaxed, letting Jack have as many packets of crisps as people would buy him. The men, as is the habit of men who drink, became louder and more garrulous as the time passed on and the beer went down and the barman, in one of his brief lulls in trade, leaned over the bar.

'Ow about showing us what he can do then?'

'That's it, come on, Tom, give us a private exhibition. There'll be room if we pull the chairs back a bit.'

Before Tom had a chance to reply his companions were busy clearing a space so he shrugged and grinned, not liking to refuse when he'd been shown such generosity and friendliness. The men settled down expectantly round the improvised ring as Tom whistled Jack to heel.

He explained, 'He doesn't do circus tricks, you know, he's a working dog.'

'That's all right, mate, we've seen 'em on the telly. Go on.'

To answer the call to heel Jack had to thread his way through the legs of spectators and he very thankfully sat close up to Tom's leg.

'Heel,' Tom commanded, and set off on a pattern of heelwork which necessitated very tight, precise turns in the confined space. The audience were appreciative, keeping up a barrage of applause and shouts of admiration.

Jack had become accustomed to the hollow booming echoes of the exhibition hall but the acoustics of the tap-room were the opposite. In the smoky atmosphere the noise was like a deadening blanket on Jack's ears, sense-dulling, claustrophobic, and by the time he'd done all the heelwork exercises and Tom was collecting items to put down for the search he was as skittish and nervous as he had ever been at a show. His thoughts of his clean, green home, away from all this senseless rumpus were very enticing.

In the short interval as Tom prepared the items for

the search, he had given permission for Jack to have another bag of crisps and a woman was feeding them to him one at a time on the palm of her hand. Because of his liking for crisps he didn't see Tom hurriedly put the comb, pen, key ring and purse he'd borrowed on the bar and make a desperate-looking exit through a door marked GENTS. He didn't realise Tom wasn't there until a clumsy passer-by trod on his tail.

Jack instinctively whipped his head round to snap at the shoe and the wearer, a recent arrival, roared, 'Bite me, would yer. Dogs shouldn't be allowed in boozers,' and kicked Jack not too gently on the rump, bringing a shower of insults upon himself. There had been no thought to harm anyone when Jack had snapped, it had simply been a reflex action and when he was kicked he looked round for Tom. Tom wasn't there. He searched around in panic but all that caught his eye was the swinging of the doors as someone went out. Tom had gone out and Jack had no intention of staying in this foreign place without him. If Tom had given him the command to 'stay' nothing short of being moved bodily would have shifted Jack, but he'd been given no orders and he was afraid without Tom.

He reached the doors before beer-dulled minds had grasped his intention, pushed with his nose and wriggled through the narrow gap as the shouts went up behind him.

'Grab that dog!'

'Hold him!'

'Don't let him get out.'

But Jack was out, hesitating on the pavement, looking for Tom. Tom wasn't there. Jack started to quarter, trying to pick up the familiar scent when the doors burst open and two men rushed at him, 'Come 'ere!'

Nothing could have been calculated to make Jack take off more quickly. He ran along the pavement to get round the nearest corner and away from the pursuing crowd who gave him crisps and kicked him at the same time. He ran aimlessly as far as his direction was concerned but all the time watching, listening and sniffing for any sign of Tom.

He lengthened his stride when the shouting men rounded the corner, still chasing him and the people he passed shrank away from him as though he was a pariah-dog with rabies instead of holding him as the following men instructed. He turned another corner, then another, the shouts of his hunters fading and dying until they were lost in the distance. He settled down then to the pace he used for long journeys, the steady lope he could maintain for hours and would maintain until he found Tom.

The traffic wasn't at its daytime volume but it got heavier as he travelled and it wasn't long before he reached the big roundabout with a statue and a fountain in the middle, a place he recognised. Tom wouldn't be far away now. Jack ran on. He ran, without thinking, out into the road and the scream of brakes, hooting of horns and yells of the pedestrians put fear into him again and the fear gave him speed to spring back to the safe pavement where he ran close to the walls of the buildings.

It was night time, but not his kind of night time, which was dark and quiet with only the wind in the trees or a hoot of a hunting owl to listen to. Here the night was brightly illuminated with harsh yellow overhead lights and it seemed as though these people never slept, there were so many of them hurrying about. But it would be all right when he found Tom. Tom made everything all right. He ran on.

Twice more he caused the cars to brake and swerve as he crossed roads and each time he ran faster to get away to where there was peace and stillness, where he would be able to take his time quartering for Tom's scent.

He came to a river. Not a river lined with grassy banks and trees, not with the water ever-changing like his own turbulent salmon streams, but a steady flowing, wide body of water which reflected the rows of street lights in its oily surface and had iron railings for banks. He stopped at the river, searching about for a way down to the water to drink, but he could find no way down so he set off eastward along the concrete banks, knowing he would pick up the scent here somewhere if Tom had been down to the river.

He trotted on for a long way, hearing the boom of a big bell, which pealed out at regular intervals, growing fainter each time.

It was very late now and he had moved away from the terror of the traffic. The streets on his right were quiet and deserted, streets that might hold Tom's trail, so he turned into them, starting to quarter again. He searched until his paws were sore with the unaccustomed pavements and until the hard going had put weariness into his indefatigable body and spirit. He gave up temporarily, looking for a place to sleep. He found a corner—he always slept in a corner—in an alley filled with dustbins. He curled up close to the wall with his nose under his tail. Early tomorrow he would find Tom.

The clangour of the dustbin lids awoke him as a man in a grubby white coat and apron upended a bucket of refuse. When the man saw Jack stretch himself he made a feinting run at him.

'*Gerroutofit yer bleedin' thing.*'

Jack dodged the swinging boot, running out to the street where he stopped to study the ground. These hard roads held no tell-tale footmarks in heavy dew or loamy surface and Tom's trail might be anywhere, but first, Jack had to drink. Food was no problem yet, he'd been fed last night and wouldn't get hungry again until evening and, indeed, could go two days without food and not suffer the ill effects a human would. But where was the water? There was the river but he'd found no way down to drink last night and anyway, that water hadn't smelled too appetising. It was only just after dawn with the streets still quiet so he went deeper into them, remembering the stone fountain. He'd be able to drink there.

He didn't find the fountain, just more and more streets, becoming increasingly filled with traffic and the noise that went with it and he didn't cross Tom's trail. At home, when he and Tom were working apart searching for traps or poachers, if he had roamed far and was late back to the Land Rover, and the Land Rover was gone, Jack simply went home and Tom was always there before him. So that's what he must do now, go home. He was already moving north and when he made his decision he carried on that way, settling down to a purposeful trot that would get him home eventually. He even forgot his need for water, for the moment. The distance he had to go meant nothing to him, in fact he couldn't comprehend what distance meant, he only knew that to keep going was to eventually arrive back at home.

The streets became denser, more compact, more dangerous with cars and he escaped road accidents narrowly on three occasions, but he kept on regardless of the increasing soreness of his pads and growing thirst. Just before noon, the character of the streets changed and now they were lined with grass verges, some even had grass running in the centre of them, there were trees and flowers in gardens. The air was less acrid and as he passed a garden gate he heard the wonderful sound of flowing, gushing, gurgling water. He went up the path. The water was pouring from a pipe fastened to the wall and was disappearing into a hole in the ground, but while it kept running Jack kept on lapping. It was bad water, grey in colour and foul tasting but it was wet and it was the only water he'd been able to find. In spite of the bad tang, it eased his thirst and he wouldn't now have to go out of his way to look for a stream. When the rushing ceased he turned about to set off north again with renewed vigour.

The further he went now, the better the going became. The houses grudgingly gave way to more and more open spaces until the open spaces won and there were no more houses, just the road which was two roads side by side with grass in the middle and hard shale banks on the outside edges. The vehicles moved very fast on this road, passing Jack with a screaming whine and a sound like a gale whistling about Scargill Croft. He crossed from the rough shale to the grass in the centre where the going was softer as his pads had begun to bleed a little, but it was all right on the grass.

He kept his eyes to the front, searching for some friendly landmark that would tell him he was nearing home, but the road stretched out before him endlessly, every mile of it just like the mile before or after. But no matter, Jack knew where he lived and there was only the space in between to cover.

When the sun was close to the horizon he dropped to the grass to rest a while, and as he lay recovering, a car with a flashing blue light on top stopped close to him. A young man in a blue suit got out and walked slowly towards Jack.

'Now then, Jack,' he said softly and kindly, 'come on then, there's the boy.'

These were the first kind words Jack had heard since he'd lost Tom. He pushed himself to his feet and walked wearily to the stranger, tongue hanging out, tail wagging. The young man squatted down to stroke him, gaining his confidence, and after a few minutes of whispered friendliness, took a good handful of Jack's collarette and opened the car door.

'In, Jack, in!'

Jack braced his feet. He didn't want to go in, he wanted to go home.

'Come on,' said the young man sternly, tugging hard. Jack warned him with a low growl and jerked away, snapping at the gripping hand. The young man let go quickly, Jack took to his heels across the road, down the hard shale bank and into the fields. The young man spoke into his radio, '... and I've just seen that champion dog that's missing, lying down as nice as you like in the middle of the M.1 ... no, he wouldn't let me put him in the car ... took off in the direction of Stockwood ... right. Out.'

There was water at the bottom of a ditch at the side of the field, but there was nothing to eat. When he'd drunk his fill he quartered the field he was in, and the next one, for rabbit but there was nothing so that night he slept hungry, curled up in a corner of the field. He badly wanted Tom and Agnes and Rex and Philip and Marjorie and Scargill Croft. But he would sleep first and go home when he was refreshed.

Chapter 7

(7)

The approach of another dog had Jack springing to his feet in the early dawn. He had slept the deep sleep of the weary, undisturbed by dreams and except for a slight tenderness of his pads was as fit and ready as ever. He spent a few moments returning the exploratory sniffs of the strange dog before going down into the ditch to drink. He hadn't eaten the previous day but his hunger wouldn't take on major proportions until his regular feeding time in the evening and he turned his face north unerringly.

At this point the road veered slightly to the west so he left that precarious route and kept to the fields. The hedges were green and thick but a short hunt always turned up some hole or gap he could squeeze through. It was better in the fields, and with thick grass covering the soft top soil he barely noticed his sore paws as he loped on and on.

He crossed streams, ditches and roads, but kept as true to his course as a homing pigeon. He saw villages in the distance and passed quite close to two of them but built-up areas held no lure for him even though there may have been a chance of getting food. All the while he kept his eyes open for rabbits but not with a great deal of hope, it being daytime when they would be in their burrows sleeping. When the sun was directly behind him he came to where the fields ended, where houses, thinly spread at first but thickening quickly, stretched away to the east and west and he knew he would have to go through this place with its noise and pad-wearing ground.

Following the pattern of all the other towns he'd seen, everything increased the farther he penetrated, traffic, people, noise, dust, and of course the air got worse with the grey vapour coming from underneath the cars. When he got to the busiest part, where everyone hurried from shop to shop and to and from bus stops, the pavements had taken their toll and he limped slowly amongst the shoppers, dry-throated, his empty belly beginning to shrink painfully, but knowing only that he had to keep on going to get home. There, there would be food and milk and his corner.

'Hello, Jack.'

He looked up at hearing his name but there was only a strange girl standing in a shop doorway—she was holding a piece of meat out to him and the saliva streamed from his jaws as he went to take it. It was a small piece that went down in one swallow, without chewing, but it was the best piece of meat Jack had ever tasted. The girl retreated into the shop and held out another piece. Jack followed, leaving bloody imprints of his paws on the tiled floor and when he swallowed the second one, the girl went through into a back room where she held out a dish of meat and the smell of it made Jack run. The desire for food was greater than the pain of his paws.

He ate greedily, wolfishly, snatching mouthfuls and swallowing them whole and when he'd emptied the dish he looked round for more but there was only water in another dish so he drank. The girl had left him alone, going out and closing the door to keep him in, so when he'd drunk all the water there was nothing to do but lie down until someone opened the door for him to go out and carry on his way home.

With his belly at least partly full and hunger pains dismissed for the time being, Jack attended to his paws, licking away the dirty blood, leaving the tender, worn pads clean. Then he slept.

Late in the afternoon the girl brought him some more water, a bar of chocolate and a visitor, her own miniature poodle.

'It won't be long now, Jack,' she said, giving him a pat, and went back to attend to her customers, leaving the dogs to make friends.

She'd spoken the truth. Hardly had Jack given the poodle a good sniffing over when the door opened again, and there was Tom. Sore paws forgotten, Jack jumped up to greet him with so much enthusiasm he nearly knocked his master over backwards and Tom laughed.

'Steady lad, steady. It's all right now.'

Jack's tail was off like a metronome at quick time and he insisted on standing with his fore-paws on Tom's chest to be stroked and tickled as he wallowed in the initial ecstasy of finding Tom.

'He *is* glad to see you,' the girl smiled over Tom's shoulder.

'Aye, it's the first time we've been separated for more than an hour or two since I got him. And it was my fault. I've been out of my mind, sitting there in London waiting to see if anyone would know him from the television report. You've got to accept the reward.'

'No, I know what it would be like if I lost Pepé. I'm glad I got the chance to hold him here for you, it was only an accident that I happened to be at the shop door when he was passing. It looks as though he was trying to get home.'

'It does that. All the way to Bedford and probably nothing to eat till you fed him. Never mind, Jack, you can have as much rabbit as you like when we get home ...' his voice dropped and he added ruefully, 'not that I'm too anxious to get *there*, for once. My missus is going to give me hell for losing him.'

They said goodbye to the girl and Tom gave her an open invitation to visit Scargill estate whenever she felt like a quiet holiday. She stood in the doorway of her shop waving like an old friend as they drove away but Jack had no eyes for her. His gaze was glued to the road before them, to the north. He knew this time he was really going home.

It was dark when they drove up to the house but the family rushed out to meet them and for a while the joy of the reunion took precedence over everything, with Agnes and the children fussing over Jack as though he'd been lost for two years rather than two days. Tom skinned one of the rabbits Ira Love had dropped in as he'd passed earlier that day, and when Jack saw him drop it in his dish that was the end of the welcome home celebrations as far as he was concerned. He got down with the whole carcass, crunching, tearing, gnawing, chewing, oblivious of everything but his own pleasure of the fresh meat, deaf to Tom's half-hearted protestations of innocence as Agnes, true to his prediction, gave him hell. She ranged from the inadvisability of allowing half-baked countrymen loose in London to the downright evil effects of drink on the human brain. She wasn't a nagging woman normally but when she considered she had just cause, she could be as shrewish as any of her sex. Tom, being a reasonable man, and having no valid defence, took his tongue-lashing docilely and was made to promise he'd never get drunk again regardless of the fact that he hadn't been drunk when he'd lost Jack. He was openly relieved when it was time for bed.

* * *

Although the next day was an ordinary working day it was like a holiday to Jack. The weather was clear and cool, promising heat later, perfect conditions for a lively dog to range, roam and run off his excess energy. As it was getting on for the time when the salmon would be jumping again, they went with Ira and Dapper along the river and up the streams, searching for signs of predators. They looked out all the old otter holts but there were no trails anywhere and Tom hoped the black killers would give Scargill a miss that year.

'Hmmm,' grumped Ira, 'I'll believe that when I see it. Y'haven't told me how you come to be separated from the dog yet, anyway.'

Tom tossed his head. 'Don't *you* start, I've had enough lecturing with Agnes last night. I thought she was never going to stop.'

'Arrrr. Well, you fellers as gets married asks for all you get!'

He let the subject drop, knowing he'd hear all about it in the Bull where Tom would no doubt make a huge joke of it all in the safety of the taproom—when he'd had a few.

When they got home that evening, Agnes was in tears with her arms round a sobbing Marjorie. Philip, being a man, sat silently at the table with a plateful of untouched food although the tears were not far from welling out of his damp eyes.

As Tom entered the room Philip blurted, 'Dad, it's Rex.'

Jack had gone to Rex's corner for the ritual of sniffed greetings but instead of his friend he found a piece of blanket with a lumpy something under it. He could smell Rex all right but the kitchen was always thoroughly laced with the scent of the old dog. Tom knelt beside Jack and slowly lifted the blanket and there was Rex, curled up, as if sleeping, but there was no movement of his ribs.

Jack sniffed all around the body, nudging the grey coat now and then to wake him up but Rex didn't move. Tom looked over his shoulder at his family.

'You'd better go watch the telly while I do this.'

Marjorie sobbed louder as her weeping mother took her, arms around her shoulders, out of the room. Philip hesitated, then followed them. Tom ran his hand the length of Rex's side.

'The old lad's gone, Jack.'

Jack looked up at the strange timbre of Tom's voice, then nosed at Rex's flank again. Tom shook his head.

'No good, Jack. Come on, let's get it over with.'

Tom carried the rigor-stiff body out of the house, down behind the chicken runs to the place where Jack had picked up the scent of his first fox. He put his burden gently down and returned to get a spade from the tool shed. He sighed many times as he dug a round hole to take the shape of the curled-up body and made noises that Jack had never heard him make before when he was shovelling the soil back to cover up Rex. Jack sat and watched. He was puzzled as to why Tom was doing this to Rex, but not worried. Anything Tom did was all right with Jack. Tom went over the hill to where there was a rocky outcrop, he made six journeys, each time bringing back as many rocks as he could carry to pile on Rex's grave. It wasn't beyond the bounds of possibility that a hungry fox would scratch away the soil to get at Rex's body for Tom knew the old tale that foxes will only eat meat which they themselves have killed, was a fallacy. *Any* animal will eat *anything* it recognises as food, providing it's hungry enough.

The atmosphere at Scargill Croft couldn't have been more miserable for the next week than if one of the humans had died and when the children, who had learned to walk by hanging on to Rex's coat, showed no signs of cheering up he effected a remedy that was killing two birds with one stone. After work, on the sixth day after Rex had died, he made a telephone call.

The following morning Jack knew he was going to another show. With the pack of sandwiches, the flask of tea and the children they drove away from a waving Agnes with her instructions not to be late back. It wasn't quite the same as the other times they'd gone to a show, as they stopped at the school in the village where the children got out.

From the pavement Philip pleaded, 'Aw, go on, Dad, tell us the surprise.'

Tom grinned tantalisingly. 'It won't be a surprise if I tell you, will it?'

His daughter tried her female way of prising it out of him. 'If you don't tell us, I won't tell you what Mam's buying you for your birthday.'

'I can wait for my birthday to find that out. *I'm* not nosey.'

Mentally she stamped her foot. 'You're rotten, Dad.'

'I know,' Tom said agreeably, slamming the door and letting out the clutch.

They drove back, passed the end of the estate track, and down into the low country with its regiments of fields where a dog couldn't run in a straight line for very far. The drive didn't last as long as Jack had expected but he wasn't sorry, although he whined his disappointment when Tom got out and left him in the Land Rover.

They had parked beside a low hedge and over the hedge Jack could see a garden. He watched Tom walk up the garden path, knock on the door of the brick house at the top, and go inside when someone opened the door. As always when Tom left him, Jack settled down with his eyes fastened on the last place he'd been able to see him. There were a lot of dogs barking in the distance somewhere behind the house but Jack hardly moved, staring at the house door as though willing Tom to come out.

It was a longish wait and when Tom finally did appear there was another man with him and Tom had something in his arms. Jack's ears pricked when he saw the black bundle move. It was a dog, a young dog. Tom opened the Land Rover door.

'Come on, Jack, let Wilf have a look at you.'

Jack was more interested in the pup than the man who'd bred him, rearing up to inspect it with the all-revealing sniff. Tom held the pup low for him to investigate and Wilf ran his hands over Jack's gleaming coat, probing the work-toughened, bulky muscles it covered.

'Aye, Tom, he's a grand 'un all right,' he chuckled. 'They're practically fightin' for Bess's pups after the write-ups the trade papers've given Jack. Seems like all the workin' dog men want a Belgian and I'd even a shepherd on the telephone who's thinking o' trying one an' I always thought it 'ud take a miracle to get them blokes off Border Collies. Looks like you've started a fashion.'

Tom inclined his head. 'Well, he's still young yet but I'll say I've never had a better dog for his age.'

He put Jack back in the Land Rover and climbed in with the pup. Wilf slammed the door and spoke to him through the open window, 'Just say you've never had a better dog full stop.'

Tom smiled, 'You might be right. See you later.'

Wilf stood back, 'You know I'm bloody well right. So-long.'

On the way home Jack got acquainted with his brother, Charles de Montpelier, Charlie to his friends. The newcomer naturally still carried the strong smell of the kennels, a smell Jack found most intriguing, incorporating as it did traces of his own mother's milk and her body, that of his other brothers and sisters whom he would never see and the strong pipe aroma which was always present on Wilf's clothing. Charlie, as Jack had been, was completely taken up by his first journey in the Land Rover, sitting in the front passenger seat, watching wide-eyed as the tops of the trees flashed past him. All the while Tom kept up the comforting flow of soft talk, starting in the first few minutes of their association to transfer the pup's affections from Bess to himself.

When Philip and Marjorie burst into the kitchen that afternoon, after running all the way from the lane's end where the school bus dropped them, they looked around eagerly for their surprise and it was Marjorie who saw the high-sided cardboard box in Rex's old corner. She looked in, shrieked, and dropped to her knees. 'Philip, it's another Jack!'

She picked up the latest addition to the Ewing household, cradling it in her arms like a baby. Philip, a year her senior, walked across to consider the pup knowingly, as befits a dog man, without a lot of childish fuss.

'Yes,' he declared, 'he's not a bad 'un. What we going to call him, Dad?'

'Charlie.'

The children looked at each other, horrified.

'Charlie?' they said simultaneously. 'Aw, Dad, not Charlie, that's not a dog's name.'

'It's *his* name,' Tom growled, keeping his face straight.

'Now kids,' Agnes said loftily, 'you know your dad deliberately picks horrible names just to tease us, you know his twisted sense of humour,' and took Charlie from her daughter's arms to give him his afternoon feed. Tom grinned at Jack who was watching from his corner.

'Come on, Jack, let's go see if the rabbits have come out to play. You could do with a run.'

The word 'rabbits' was magic to Jack. It conjured up the

thrill of the chase, the battle of craft to drive the quarry where he wanted it, the satisfaction of a clean kill and, the best thing, his favourite meat for his evening meal. He was at the door before Tom, who turned to say sternly, 'And don't you lot be spoiling that pup when I've gone—and don't forget his name, will you?'

A chorus of low, but decidedly derisive remarks, accompanied his exit.

Charlie fitted into life at Scargill as neatly as Jack had done. He was Agnes's charge for the first few weeks in which she house-trained him and taught him the very elementary rudiments of obeying simple commands so that when, at three months, Tom started him on a simple daily obedience lesson, he was able to sit, lie down, and answer to the recall unless there was anything of particular interest holding his attention. Tom said that at that stage he was showing all the early promise Jack had done, although it was too much to expect consecutive dogs of Jack's calibre even from the same parents. Jack, unlike old Rex, welcomed a playmate. He still wasn't two years old and liked nothing better than to run free, rolling and tumbling with one of his own kind, and then escorting his underling back to Tom when he recalled them, escorting that consisted of many rough prods of the nose to keep Charlie going in the desired direction.

In the spring, just after Jack's second birthday, they went to the first open-air show of the year—Tom never bothered with the indoor winter ones—and Jack watched Charlie take second place in the Novice class. It was a blustery day of intermittent showers and Tom was satisfied with the result, telling Agnes the offputting weather had depleted the chances of more experienced dogs than Charlie. For Jack, such a thing as the weather might never have existed. To him, rain, sleet, snow, winds and heat-waves were there to be ignored. Whatever moods the elements decided to adopt made not the slightest difference to the job in hand. So while 'amateur' dogs, some of whom were very highly trained, slunk about with wet coats thinking only about getting home to a warm fire, Jack the 'professional' was on the mark to search for and find a bunch of keys and a handkerchief with the same diligence as if they were rabbits or poachers. He walked away with the 'C' Test and bellied down in the crowded 'restaurant' marquee to enjoy a pork pie and a chocolate biscuit, his reward.

Tom and Agnes were gratefully cupping their hands around beakers of hot tea whilst the children, who were also, apparently, immune to the weather, took Jack and Charlie to the exercise area. A middle-aged woman, grey-haired and shrewd-eyed pushed her way through the mass.

'Been looking for you all over, Tom. How're you keeping, Agnes?'

'Fine, thanks, Eveline, how's yourself?'

Eveline Montgomery ran what were probably the most famous kennels in Europe. She specialised, and made her living from breeding Alsatians for the show ring but her first love was obedience and the list of her successful dogs was long and impressive. She was, as many women are, a brilliant handler and the equal of any man when it came to training a dog. She was not, though, renowned for indulging in small talk and as Tom expected she didn't waste any time in getting down to business.

'You can guess what I want?'

Tom could guess but he shook his head.

She said, 'I want to make you an offer for Jack.'

Agnes laughed. 'You're not serious, Eveline?' Eveline was always serious.

Tom said, 'Let's hear it.'

Agnes frowned. 'Tom,' she said softly but ominously,

quite aware of the sky-high prices a breeder would pay for an exceptional dog, but hardly believing Tom would even listen to a proposition which would entail the selling of Jack. Eveline ignored Agnes's protective indignation, making her offer quickly and briefly with no mincing of words. It was what Tom had expected. He agreed.

Three weeks of the normal working routine passed fairly uneventfully, the only alteration to established procedure being the introduction of Charlie to the team. As with Jack, Tom broke him in steadily to the livestock, always keeping him on the lead until he was sure he could trust him not to stampede cattle or sheep or attack any of the new lambs or go chasing after the small herds of roe deer. There was one incident which almost ended nastily and stickily for Charlie when he went too close to an old roebuck. The buck was guarding his does and fawns and charged the inquisitive pup without warning. Although the roes are a miniature of their species, those small sharp antlers, coming at speed, could have made a nasty hole in the young dog. But Charlie dodged the first charge and when the buck turned, Jack was there to bark and send him away. Jack, as big as the buck, was a different opponent from an ungainly pup and it retreated with what dignity it could maintain.

Unexpectedly Tom took them home at lunchtime one day and Agnes had been expecting them; she had a meal ready for Tom. As he ate, Agnes took out Jack's brush and started carefully grooming him. Tom swallowed a mouthful of hot potato.

'What difference is that going to make?'

Agnes brushed away vigorously. 'He ought to look nice today.'

'It's not what he looks like that matters.'

'It might, you never know, she might like him more.'

Instead of remarking on the illogicality of women, Tom ate a piece of steak pie.

Eveline Montgomery was on time, parking her van outside the house as Tom finished his after-lunch smoke. Charlie, much to his displeasure, was shut in the tool shed and Jack left in the kitchen, every hair in place, when Tom and Agnes went out to Eveline. Eveline was opening the back doors of the van and a beautiful dog jumped out. It was a full Collie with a long, well-groomed brown and white coat and the thin, aristocratic face of the breed.

'Isn't she lovely,' Agnes breathed.

Eveline, in her clipped way, said, 'As it happens she is, but it wouldn't make any difference if she was as ugly as sin. She's the finest obedience bitch I've ever had and I've been saving her for someone like your Jack. I'll found a new strain, bred purely for obedience if I die in the attempt. The Border Collies have had it all their own way for too long.'

She was referring to what is considered to be the most highly trainable of all breeds by the majority of people in the dog world. A breed that has no Kennel Club standards and therefore cannot be shown simply for beauty, but a dog very quick to learn to obey commands. Many shepherds owe their livelihood to the Border Collies.

Tom stroked the well-groomed head and held his hand out to be sniffed delicately. 'Now then, girl, they've tarted you up for your wedding day as well by the look of you but I don't think Jack'll notice,' he laughed. 'You won't be so immaculate when he's finished with you.'

'There's no need,' Agnes said icily, 'to be vulgar. In fact, it might be as well if you take Charlie out and let me and Eveline attend to this.'

Tom roared and slapped his thigh. 'You're joking. I wouldn't miss this for the world. Got to make sure my lad can do his stuff when the chips are down.'

Eveline slipped a choker over the bitch's head. 'If he's as coarse as you I shouldn't think he'll have any trouble. Heel, Rhona.'

They took her round to the back yard to let her sniff and accustom herself to the surroundings and Jack stood up with his paws on the kitchen sink watching, unblinking, as if he knew there was something special in the air. They walked Rhona about for half an hour, letting her pick up Jack's scent before they were introduced. 'If we don't let him out soon he'll be coming through the window, glass an' all,' Tom said.

Jack hadn't moved since he'd seen the strangers. He stood nearly five feet tall, his head framed in the window above the lace curtain, triangular ears pricked, his collarette ruffed out, showing at his most attractive.

Eveline agreed. 'Bring him then, and I'll say this, not that it matters, they will make a damn fine handsome pair. Let's hope the pups inherit the best points of both.'

When Tom opened the door, Jack didn't have to be coaxed out, he came running, and Eveline slipped the choker off Rhona so she could go to meet him.

'Look who's come to see you, Jack,' cooed Agnes, slightly pink-faced.

'That's the stuff, lad,' Tom leered. 'Don't waste any time.'

'Tom Ewing, if you don't ...'

'Let the little boy be,' Eveline cut in on Agnes's admonition, 'he's got to find out the mystery of life sooner or later.'

Tom hadn't got his own back for the rousting Agnes had given him when Jack had got lost and he was enjoying himself immensely at her expense.

'Go on, Jack, get to it, show these women what you're made of.'

What Jack was seeing was another dog, a playmate to take

Charlie's place, Charlie who was whining loudly in the toolshed. Jack pranced up to the Collie to exchange nose sniffs and then made little jumps to the right and left, wanting her to play at chasing. All she did was move closer to him and stand, just looking. Jack made a quick sprint of a few yards, then ran back to touch her nose with his. He repeated this invitation four times but all the lethargic Collie would do was come up to stand nose to nose.

Agnes smiled. 'He's courting her, isn't it nice.'

Tom ran a hand through his hair, 'Courting her! He's as daft as a brush, that's what he is. Get on with it, dog!'

Eveline tut-tutted. 'Give 'em time. I've been mating dogs nearly thirty-five years now and I can tell you they don't all know what to do. Sometimes you've to show 'em.'

About then the seasonal smell of the bitch started to penetrate and Jack started to explore to find out what was different about her. His curiosity and excitement increased by the second and the moment it was clear he knew what was expected of him, Agnes steered Tom, with a series of not too gentle pushes to the kitchen door.

'Inside,' she said in a tone that would take no denial, 'and we'll make Eveline a cup of tea.'

'But,' Tom started.

'No buts,' Agnes finished and pushed him in, leaving Eveline alone to witness the consummation. Agnes even drew the kitchen curtains.

'No one would ever believe you were bred and born in the country,' Tom said sadly.

'Whereas,' quoted his wife, '*anyone* would believe you were born in a sewer. Put the kettle on while I make some sandwiches.'

Chapter 8

(8)

Tom had guessed right in that one couldn't expect two dogs of the same calibre from the same parents, but that was mainly because Jack was an exceptional dog by any standards. At two years old, Charlie was an excellent working dog, one many farmers or gamekeepers would have snapped up if he'd been put on the market. Like Jack, he'd learned quickly and well all the lore of estate life and could track and search with the best.

What he did lack was Jack's precision in the obedience ring and in that exacting company it isn't sufficient for a dog to obey a command promptly and willingly. He must sit, stand or lie at precisely the correct angle as required by the particular exercise or have marks deducted if he fails to do this. He got a fair share of first prizes, but just as many seconds and thirds and sometimes he wasn't even in the running if he had had an off day.

However, it was his work at home that mattered and as he did that reliably enough, it was all right by Tom. As Jack had won everything it was possible for him to win, more than once, Tom retired both dogs from competition when Jack was four.

Rhona had produced a fine litter of five dogs and one bitch from her first meeting with Jack, and had been brought back to him on two subsequent occasions and Eveline had no trouble at all in selling the pups of two champions. These weren't the only ventures Jack had into fatherhood. Wilf had bred a rather small bitch who, apart from her lack of size, measured up as a perfect specimen of a Belgian Sheepdog. Jack's aid was recruited and willingly given, in an attempt to add stature to her pups. Again the breeding experiment worked and Wilf's bitch became a twice-yearly visitor to Scargill Croft. In stud fees and prize money, Jack wiped out the deficiency of the price Tom had paid both for him and Charlie, vet's fees included, and was showing a handsome profit when Tom called it a day for them in competition.

Their life was ideal for dogs. Good hard exercise all day at work, a hearty meal at the end of it and, when the evenings were light enough, fun after dinner catching rabbits. Jack's tastes had developed with his years and after much prompting from Tom, had acquired a real liking for mild beer. He was a great favourite in the Bull and it was argued seriously whether or not he had a capacity and head for drink the equal of the late Rex.

That year Tom would always remember as the year of the thieves and never was any man so thankful for having two competent assistants. It seemed to Tom as though every kind of game robber, from every part of Britain had descended on Scargill with one accord.

They even had a Golden Eagle, a species never seen in that area as far as living memory stretched back. Ira was first to sight it as it took off to fly east with the long tail of a pheasant hanging from its talons. Where it had its eyrie, they'd no idea. It was said that an eagle will think nothing of a fifty-mile flight when searching for food for its young and even if they'd known where the bird was nesting, the Golden Eagle is a protected animal. Tom scratched his head; he was going to have trouble getting rid of it if it realised what a well stocked larder Scargill was.

Then there were the foxes with their cubs to feed but with trackers like Jack and Charlie, Tom soon whittled them down to acceptable proportions, the dogs searching out the dens in the daytime and Tom waiting in the nearest cover with his shotgun for the killers to come out into the moonlight. Six fine brushes decorated the walls of his study.

The otters were work for the dogs alone. When Dapper had died, six months after Rex, Ira Love had insisted that he be replaced with a dog of his own choosing and had found another mongrel, paid for by the estate, a small, hairy, fearless fellow who looked as though he had a good dash of Cairn in him and his terrier qualities showed up in the way he took to diving into holts to chase the otters out. Having done that, his part of the hunt was over, although he always followed Jack and Charlie, ever ready to do battle but he hadn't the legs to keep up.

Tom had devised a good strategy that failed very rarely, only the wiliest otters escaped the death-dealing jaws of the two Belgians. Tom and Ira would wait on opposite banks of the stream and Jack and Charlie would go into the water, downstream from the holt. In the upper reaches, the water was mostly shallow and the shallower the better. The Belgians would stand chest deep into the current and watch Yapper—a most suitable name—go into the mouth of the holt. If the holt was in use it wasn't long before a black flash would slide into the stream, and the hunt was on. It was Jack and Charlie's job to surge forward noisily, driving the otter upstream until the water was so shallow it had no choice but to take the suicidal step of trying to get away over land. From the top of the banks the men could see the gliding black body tacking from bank to bank seeking a chance to streak between the barking, splashing dogs. If he looked like succeeding, a charge of shot aimed a yard or two in front of him would drive him back and the farther they pushed him, the upshelving bottom and narrowing banks lessened his chances of eluding death. For, once he left the water, he was finished. As water creatures go otters are not slow on the ground and although the final result of the chase was always predictable, it didn't lessen the dogs' enjoyment. Jack administered the *coup-de-grâce* three times, Charlie twice, and two old dog otters, secure in the knowledge that they were the kings of the water, slipped quickly downstream to the safety of the river.

Men too had to be dealt with that year, silent men, skilful and almost totally undetected. Jack came back to the Land Rover, from a solo patrol, carrying a dead partridge. It was clear the bird's neck had been expertly wrung. Tom dropped it in the back of the Land Rover and got out his shotgun. 'Seek, Jack.'

With Charlie at Tom's heel, Jack backtracked to the spot where he'd found the partridge.

'Seek!' Tom ordered.

The dogs started to quarter, Tom standing back as they moved outward, noses nearly touching the ground. They didn't know they were looking for signs of the poachers, only that they were to indicate anything they discovered that was out of place, that shouldn't have been on the estate. Charlie passed one place, then went back to it to give it a more thorough examination. He'd found a footprint in the damp ground, in a little hollow that held rainwater after a downpour, a place where the earth was always a little muddy. The marks of a gumboot stood out clearly. Tom touched the imprint with his finger.

'Seek!'

Both dogs nosed at the ridged impression and started to quarter again but this time they knew what they were looking for and picked up the scent very quickly. If Tom had let them both go they'd have been out of sight in seconds leaving him to flounder along in the hope of catching up later so he kept Charlie with him to track Jack and let Jack race on in front unhindered. It was a long track, right down to the river and there they found evidence that the bow of a small boat had been pulled up on to the bank. Tom had expected to be led to one of the gates of the estate, but the way the poacher, or poachers, had come in showed they were inventive if nothing else. Tom would have to be equally clever to catch them. He went home for a few hours' sleep.

The vigil that night was fruitless and at three o'clock in the morning he gave up. Either the poachers weren't coming or they'd entered the estate by another way. As they drove slowly home, black clouds built up from the west to touch the moon and finally cover it and the first pea-sized raindrops spattered noisily on the metal roof.

The rain didn't stop that day and from the kitchen window the surrounding hills were indistinct through the grey slashing sheets. Tom pulled on an oilskin jacket and old sou'wester as Agnes packed his bag with flasks of tea and sandwiches. It was eight o'clock and almost dark. She shook her head.

'You want your head looking at, Tom Ewing. The poachers'll have more sense than you. *They* won't come out on a night like this.'

Tom heaved the bag over his shoulder. 'Come on, Jack, Charlie. If they're doin' what I think they are, this is exactly the night they will come. Goodnight.'

She reached her cheek up for a kiss. 'Goodnight then, but be careful.'

They left the Land Rover and walked the last mile in soaking blackness and settled down in a stand of spruce downwind from where the boat had landed in case the poachers used a dog. It was a dreary wait and even after the rain had stopped at ten, there was a steady plunking of big drops on his stiff oilskin from the saturated trees.

It was after midnight when he heard voices carrying clearly across the water and he put a hand on the dogs' muzzles as they raised their heads.

'Stay,' he said softly, 'stay.'

The moon was a luminous blob behind the low ceiling of shifting clouds, giving no light of any value but the creak of the rowlocks gave away the boat's position and Tom could just make out the shape as it came into the bank. Jack could see it easily, and the two men, one rowing and one in the stern.

The men splashed into the shallows as they pulled the bow out of the water and set off up the bank, their silhouettes showing vaguely for an instant against the grey sky. Tom gave them ten minutes' start and would have given them longer if the night had been dry. But if it started to rain again a downpour could ruin the scent.

Tonight, for the first time in years, Jack was wearing the tracking harness. He moved twenty feet in advance of Tom at the extent of the rope and Tom kept Charlie at heel. The trail remained so easy to follow that the rope remained taut all the way and not once did he lose it and have to waste time quartering. So swiftly did they cover the ground that Tom halted after a mile for fear of catching up the men before they started work. He waited another ten minutes and sent Jack off again.

'Seek!'

Tom admitted grudgingly that these men didn't lack confidence; they went three miles into the estate before commencing activities, right into the country of thickets and undergrowth the game birds liked to inhabit. He spotted them as he followed Jack over the crest of a low ridge; he could see a torch about a quarter of a mile away.

He sensed rather than saw some hurried moving about, then the torch was switched off and he sent Jack on again. The light reappeared to the right of where he'd seen it the first time and being nearer, he heard the quick trample of men in the undergrowth and a controlled but exultant exclamation.

'Gorrem both!'

Tom moved forward again, the dogs panting with excitement, knowing they were on some kind of a hunt. It was almost impossible to move silently through the scrub, which was becoming denser by the yard, but the men were so engrossed in their task, they failed to hear the snap of a twig and rustle of leaves.

Tom got to within twenty yards of them, turned on his own powerful torch and shouted, 'All right, stay where you are. I've got two dogs, and a gun I'm willing to use if you move.'

'Christ,' one of them said, 'it's Ewin'.'

His companion called, 'Keep hold o' them dogs, mate, I don't want worryin' wi' one o' them bastards.'

More than a little fame of the Belgians had spread around the county. Each time a story of Tom Ewing's dogs was repeated, a little was added until people who did not know them credited them with super canine qualities, believing them to be a mixture of wolves, bloodhounds and greyhounds with the ferocity of the mythical hounds of the Baskervilles and the mental power of humans.

Tom had no intention of disillusioning anyone. He said harshly, 'Stand still and the dogs won't touch you. What's that you've got?'

'A net.'

'Throw it between us.'

The light coloured bundle fluttered and fell in the torchlight.

'Fetch it, Jack.'

It was a very light but extremely strong, fine-meshed nylon net, square in shape and weighted around the edges with lead shot. Ira had spoken years before of a poacher he'd known in Norfolk who used this method but it was the first time Tom had ever seen it. To use it, it was necessary to know exactly where the birds were, which suggested that these men had scouted the estate in daylight or had at least made a careful study with powerful binoculars. During heavy rain, for some reason—most likely because pheasants are nervous and dislike the noise of the rain hitting the leaves—the birds roost on the ground instead of in the trees and the sudden glare of a torch startles them into raising their heads and giving themselves away. Before they can take evasive action the net is cast, effectively holding them down while the poachers walk in and wring their necks. At the expense of a soaking, the poachers work silently, not risking the sudden noise of a shotgun fetching the gamekeeper out of his bed.

Tom gave them a choice. They could either prove their identity to him or have a long walk to the village where he would hand them over to the policeman. Had it not been for the presence of the dogs they would have undoubtedly risked running off in separate directions, taking the chance of being stung with a few pellets. As it was they fished in their pockets, one producing a driving licence and the other final demands from the Electricity and Gas Boards. Tom memorised the names and addresses.

'All right, away you go—no, leave the bag and the net.'

They trudged off into the darkness and Tom found five birds in the bag. At the speed they worked they'd have chopped down the gamebird population to alarming proportions if he hadn't caught them—or rather, if the dogs hadn't caught them.

By the time the salmon started to come up the river

that year, Tom was breathing easily again, pretty sure he'd cleared out the bulk of the marauders, particularly pleased about the otters they'd caught and well satisfied with the number of shooting and fishing permits he'd issued. The estate ought to show a decent profit after all. But he had one more hurdle to clear.

He first got wind of it on the television newscast. Sheep farmers to the north of the estate were spending nights on end trying to catch a renegade dog, a sheep-killer living wild in the hills, but at the time of that report had succeeded in doing no more than sighting it twice. Apart from that, the only evidence that it existed was the dead sheep it left behind.

This one wasn't a dog gone crazy, a mad thing who instinctively attacked any flock it saw and slaughtered every animal it could catch simply from a blood lust drive. This was a rarer specimen, quite likely a once well looked after working dog which had been driven by circumstances to fend for itself. It only killed perhaps every two days and then simply to eat, a fact proved by the evidence that it never killed more than one sheep at a time. This dog had reverted to the wild state of its ancestors and its latent, primeval instincts of survival had come to the fore with a vengeance. It was, according to the report, as sly and cunning as any fox or wolf, and with its higher intelligence, infinitely harder to trap.

It had made its first appearance as a killer far to the north, seventy or eighty miles away from Scargill but seemed to be working on a steady southerly course for some reason and provided it kept to the same direction would undoubtedly be making an unwelcome appearance on the estate. But it was no good worrying about what might never happen and Tom put the possibility out of his mind. When the first snow fell in early November he'd forgotten it completely.

Because of its altitude rather than its northerliness, Scargill always received more than its fair share of snow and by the middle of the month the estate resembled, in a smaller way, the country to the south of Hudson's Bay. The grass was hidden away from the deer by a sparkling, six-inch deep covering of blinding white and the weather side of trunks and branches were embellished with wind-hardened snow. The first hard sample of winter was usually sudden and brutal but, thankfully, temporary. The snow could be counted upon to have made a partial disappearance well before Christmas, leaving plenty of green patches on which the roe deer could graze. But while the arctic conditions lasted, the wild creatures had to be 'spoon fed', as Tom put it. Although small, the little animals are extremely hardy and it's doubtful if any would have perished, but Tom didn't want herds of skeletons when the spring came and so took fodder out to them in a trailer towed by the Land Rover.

The dogs revelled in the snappy, icy conditions, the invigorating air, exhaled in white plumes from damp noses, encouraging them to enjoy the rough knockabout games of puppyhood. They'd take it in turns. First they'd face each other, keyed up and poised for flight, tongues lolling, brown eyes bright, almost wild with canine humour and fun, then Jack would hare away at full stretch, covering the madly pursuing Charlie with back-kicked snow until Charlie out-manoeuvred him and thudded into his shoulder, bowling him over in a shower of scattered crystals. They'd pant for a minute, toe the line, feinting with little jerky jumps to the right and left, then Charlie would break and Jack would be after him, barking his exhilaration. Tom would shout and cheer from the crawling Land Rover.

Every couple of hundred yards Tom would stop to drop a bale of hay from the trailer and look back to see the deer walk timidly from the trees to eat. He was working the southern slopes of Bracken Hill which was the most northerly part of the estate, the great Crag black and forbidding in the clear light, when he saw the blood. The bright red patch stood out more clearly than the spot on the Ace of Hearts, fifty yards away at the foot of a tall pine tree. Tom whistled the recall for the dogs and trudged nearly knee deep to look at what was left of the tragedy.

The victim had been one of that year's fawns and was now a pathetic corpse with long, bony legs, frozen stiff and straight. As Tom crunched up, a crow flapped away hurriedly and there was the quick rustle of retreating bodies under the brittle bracken, stoat maybe or weasel. A good portion of the throat had been torn out and eaten as had the exposed left shoulder and rump; the killer was choosy and preferred the better cuts of venison. The stoats or weasel—or possibly rats—weren't, or had different tastes; they had gnawed a hole in the underbelly to get at the entrails and other offal, the parts that were easily detached and carried away.

Jack and Charlie sniffed round the carcass hungrily but recognised the dead fawn as food forbidden to them. The tracks of the killer stood out clearly, the shadowed indentations tracing a dotted black line up and over the shoulder of Bracken Hill and, Tom guessed, off the estate property. He sent the dogs away, got the shotgun from the Land Rover and followed.

When he reached the curve of the hill he was about halfway from the flatland to the summit and sure enough the tracks led under the boundary wire to be lost in the thick, moorland bracken on the other side. Jack and Charlie had no respect for boundaries, they'd been told to seek and they were seeking, following the trail unerringly, careless of the roughening terrain, forging into what was National Parkland. Tom put his fingers to his lips and shrilled the recall. He didn't want some harassed, agitated sheep farmer mistaking them for the renegade and emptying his twelve bore into them. A little thought would have to go into catching and killing the culprit, a menace to every stock owner in the district.

Tom recruited Ira and Ned White and they held their council in the taproom of the Bull.

'Well,' Ira said slowly, 'if this 'ere dog's gone right back to nature he'll have gorged hisself last night and won't start gettin' hungry again till tomorrow but whether it be today or tomorrow afore he wants to eat again he'll come back to where he found easy pickings, that's certain. An' it looks as though we'll be doin' a bit o' night work.'

Ned grimaced. 'That'll be nice.'

Tom grinned. 'Do you good, and we'd better start tonight just in case.'

'Aye,' Ira agreed dourly.

According to the old gamekeeper, dogs, like many other wild animals, are creatures of habit, and as this one had found what it would consider to be an easy hunting ground the odds were it would come back to exactly the same place and by the same route.

By the time Tom's watch was showing midnight, the half moon was high enough to give reasonable light and from the Land Rover, hidden by the side of a copse and well covered with branches, they could see the tracks of the dog clearly. It hadn't snowed that day.

It was a long, long night. The dogs slept, unconcerned, in the back and the men took turns at dozing and watching. Armed as they were with sandwiches, tea, coffee and rum they were still stiff, aching and frozen when Ned shook Tom awake at six o'clock.

'Come on, Tom, your turn—unless you want to call it a day. He can't be comin' now, Ira said it'd be tonight.'

Tom groaned and stretched his arms as far as the

cramped space would allow. 'We might as well wait till daylight now, no good taking a chance on missing him.'

Ned groaned and snuggled into the hood of his parka. Tom bent below window level to light his pipe and shielded the glowing bowl with his cupped right hand. He listened to his companions breathing as he switched his gaze over the Christmassy scene to keep himself awake.

He didn't have to try to keep his lids up any more when he saw the longtailed shadow flitting over the bracken as it approached the boundary wire deceptively fast. He slowly lowered his pipe to the floor and sat perfectly still, fascinated by the confident way the dog ran without breaking its stride under the bottom strand to pass within fifty yards of the vehicle. He didn't move at once. There would be no difficulty in following the trail and he wanted the killer to get beyond the point of no return before risking scaring it with the noise of the Land Rover doors opening. He gave it three minutes' start when it would be at least a half mile into the estate, then shook his companions.

'Come on, then, let's go get him.'

They moved forward as previously planned, Ned and Ira on the flanks and the dogs between them and Tom, spaced at one hundred yard intervals so they covered a front of a quarter mile.

Jack had never hunted in that formation before but he grasped the implication and ploughed through the snow eagerly, sensing the prospect of a chase and kill. Tom kept the dogs in position easily, by dropping them flat when they got too far ahead.

The first deer would quite likely be in the vicinity of the nearest of the bales of hay and the wild dog would track them to wherever the herd had taken shelter for the night, unless he caught wind of his own hunters first and took flight.

The moon was well down, the pale light waning, when there was a crashing of bodies in a thicket to the left of the centre of the line of approach. The marauder had found another meal and a herd of ten deer, led by the buck, smashed from the trees to race directly at Ned. The buck saw him, wheeled, and the family vanished into the night. There was no need for caution now, the dog had attacked again and they had gained too much ground on him, were too close for him to break through the line and in the darkness he wouldn't know how far the line extended in each direction. Tom whistled for his dogs' attention and swung his right arm upward and forward.

'Fetch him Jack, Charlie,' he shouted. 'Fetch him.'

The panic-stricken emergence of the roe deer and the rustle of the short fight inside the thicket had keyed the already tensed-up dogs into hair trigger reaction, and the words were hardly out of Tom's mouth before they were belting into the bushes. They didn't have to look for the killer, the smell of fresh blood acting on them as efficiently as any electronic homing device.

When Jack burst into the small clearing, the killer dog was crouched defensively over a doe, the one terrible wound in the throat of the dead beast speaking volumes for its executioner's skill. In a light so faint that human eyes would have been hard pressed to make out anything at all, Jack quickly took in every detail. In all his travels around the national dog world he'd never seen one like this before. A little higher than himself at the withers, with a shorter coat, it was spare and rangy, light in colour with a curious, well-defined spine, but whatever his breed he was showing no fear. He had killed the doe and it was his to defend against all others, excluding man. He knew the threat of the most powerful animal in the world, he knew about the guns to which he had no defence, but the voice of the man he'd heard was not there in the clearing, only another dog, and another somewhere in the bushes coming closer.

Jack heard Charlie coming in on his left, so he circled to the right, answering the killer's warning growl with drawn lips and his own fearsome snarl. Charlie didn't take stock when he came upon the scene. He saw the dead doe and the culprit facing Jack and leapt forward to mete out justice.

The instant the strange dog whipped round to face the new threat, Jack launched himself and with two great bounds had his teeth in the enemy's neck, dragging him down, and Charlie was in with slashing teeth, trying for the throat. But the outlaw could fight and his lean, wiry body bent, twisted and thrashed so violently that he shook Jack off and bowled Charlie over. One dog he would have faced unflinchingly and fought to the death for the prize of the dead doe, but he hadn't survived alone for the past months by taking chances and his instinct told him his only hope of survival lay in out-distancing his attackers. As Jack came at him again he shot into the bushes, powerful jaws snapping inches behind him, and started for his hillside retreat to the north. Charlie had bounced back as though attached to a rubber band and with only six yards from the killer's nose to Charlie's tail, the three dogs twisted through the undergrowth in a death race. The outlaw could not only fight, he could run too.

They burst out on to the clear, snow-covered ground like frantic greyhounds chasing a hare and the butts of three shotguns smacked into shoulders. Tom sighted, but his own dogs were too close to risk a shot.

'*Down!*' he yelled and the years of obedience training paid off again. Jack and Charlie dropped so quickly that their momentum carried them skating forward on the crisp surface, and at the sound of Tom's voice the killer turned at right angles to run to the east. Tom sighted again, swinging the barrel smoothly to his left, leading on his target's head, and when his gun cracked the running dog cartwheeled and crashed on his back into the snow. He whimpered and moved his legs jerkily until Ned, who was nearest, walked up and put another charge of shot into his brain from point blank range. Men and dogs gathered round the corpse, the dogs sniffing at the bloody, pulped head and the men thankfully lighting tobacco.

Ned blew out a cloud of smoke. 'He's a big 'un. New 'un on me, an' all.'

'Looks like a Ridgeback,' Ira offered. 'Don't see many of 'em round here.'

The Rhodesian Ridgeback, bred for hunting the big game of Africa, is a rare dog in Britain.

Tom bent to make a fuss of Jack and Charlie for the excellent job they'd done and said, 'Good as these two are, I'm glad neither of 'em had to face him alone, they might have beaten him but he'd have made a hell of a mess of 'em. Wonder where he came from.'

'That,' Ira growled, 'is something you're not likely to find out. No one's goin' to admit owning him and have the farmers on their backs for the price of the sheep he's killed.'

'That's true,' Tom agreed, 'and most likely he belonged to some tinkers or gipsies, somebody on the road, anyway. But he doesn't belong to anyone now ... poor sod.'

Chapter 9

(9)

With the years, Jack's superb senses were tempered by a mature steadiness fostered by the eternal presence of Tom's thoughtfulness and commonsense. In the autumn of his eighth year he was a corner of a perfect working partnership with Tom and Charlie, part of a team which had kept the Scargill estate freer of thieves than at any time in its history. Tom often boasted that there had never been such a good all-round dog as Jack and that Charlie wasn't far behind. Blazing summer or freezing winter would see them covering the estate, hounding foxes into range of Tom's gun, running flushed-out otters into the ground or sniffing out the snares of the very few poachers intrepid enough to sneak on to Scargill land. Barely a day passed that didn't see them hunting, tracking or merely quartering hopefully for miscreants. It was Tom's constant vigilance, passed on to the dogs, which kept the estate's finances so healthily sound and assured him of continued employment.

The first slender thread of affection, forged on the day Jack was bought, by Tom's continual stream of reassuring talk on the way home in the Land Rover, had been woven by the years into an unbreakable, almost tangible bond. There was an affinity between Jack and Tom bordering on telepathy, a mutual understanding which had many renowned dog handlers shaking their heads in wonderment mixed with a little sneaking envy. Although they had retired from participation in obedience shows, they were invited quite regularly to give demonstrations at galas and fêtes and Tom rarely turned down an opportunity to show off and do a bit of silent boasting. He considered he had something to boast about.

After the spring, when the fawns had to be guarded along with the young pheasants and partridges, the autumn was the busiest time of the year. The big, leaping, delicious salmon with no defence against net or fish-eating carnivore required constant protection and attention. Before the big run started, all the old otter holts were checked and the land adjacent to the streams and river banks searched for signs of an influx of the whiskered killers. Some years were nearly otter free but sometimes they would descend on Scargill in families, the dog and bitch giving the cubs their final lessons in self-preservation and the art of hunting before sending them off to fend for themselves. A pair of adults with two well-grown young ones could wreak havoc in the salmon breeding beds, killing the worn out, weary females before they had time to lay the eggs.

That year Philip had worked all summer on the estate before starting at university and most days had taken Charlie with him to scout the area in which he was planting saplings, laying the foundations of new copses to attract the game birds to the southern part of the estate, for the dogs could not only work in harmony but as individuals too. As ever, Jack went with Tom in the Land Rover and they went up to the north-west corner to check the last of the streams from the river to the foot of Bracken Crag where the water tinkled over gravel beds, too shallow for the big Atlantic salmon.

Tom left the Land Rover where the track petered out

half a mile from the stream, about halfway from the source to the river, and climbed out on to the dew wet grass.

'Come on then, Jack, let's get on with it. It's Friday, y'know, an' we don't want to be late for the Bull tonight, do we?'

Jack's tail wagged at the mention of the inn. Charlie had remained a strict teetotaller, but according to Tom, Jack could drink enough mild beer for both of them. Tom picked up his shotgun and they started on the long trek.

Steadily they worked down the south bank, the man letting the dog set the pace and waiting patiently as Jack spent time investigating clumps of bushes or undercut banks that might offer refuge to an otter. But there were no tracks all the way down to the river and as he paddled them across the wide mouth of the stream in an old skiff, Tom shook his head. 'It's hard to believe, old son, but I'm beginning to think you an' that mate of yours have scared all the otters away for good. And if you have, what are you goin' to do for a bit of fun in the future?'

Jack 'grinned' and thumped the side of the little boat with his ever eager tail.

The north bank was less interesting with not so many trees and possible hidey holes, and as the heather-covered slopes of Bracken Crag loomed closer it became of less interest still, just a shallow bank rising to unbroken moorland which lifted away to the base of the stark rocks of the Crag.

At two o'clock, when they crossed the stream again by the stepping stones on the gravel beds, Tom was humming deep in his throat, contented. They'd had a clear round, it was Friday, he'd be back home before five or half past and parking outside the Bull at eight. He'd go tomorrow to see how Philip was progressing with his planting and then he'd have to check the boundary fence with Ned and authorise any necessary repairs, and Ira had asked him to put his feelers out for a new dog as Yapper was starting to feel his age and it was time to start breaking in another one.

It was a pleasant day, not too hot but bright and clear, and Tom walked with a swing, letting the affairs of estate management run through his mind, not taking any particular notice of his surroundings. Jack was away on in front inspecting the waterside mud for tracks and pushing into any undergrowth that might conceal an enemy.

Tom checked his watch. Three o'clock and he was making better time than he'd expected. He started to whistle a low tune as he came round a bend where the path had left the steepening stream bank to bypass a dense thicket but his whistling died and he halted when he saw Jack. Jack was lying perfectly still, head flat down on his paws, ears pricked. He was on a hummock ten yards back from the bank watching the water. Tom remained as still as the dog, searching the rippling surface, and then he saw it, a graceful, swift, black torpedo moving steadily upstream as it tacked from bank to bank hunting for fish. The first otter for months.

Here the stream was six feet deep and thirty feet wide, the otter's perfect element where he was lord and master of all, fish, men or dogs, and he knew it. Jack and Tom knew it too, so they stayed in position and hoped for a change in the situation. If the otter came across trout he would kill and feed there, close to the deep water and they would have little chance of taking him, but if the fishing was thin and the otter hungry—otters always seem to be hungry—he'd carry on with his search until dark, moving always upstream to the shallow reaches where they might be able to drive him from the water; if they got him on dry ground there was no question about the end result. He would be a dead otter.

Tom wished now that he had Charlie along, for with the dogs working as a team the job would be over cleanly and simply but Jack, as good as he was, couldn't be in two places at the same time and the business was going to be a drawn-out affair.

The otter was now criss-crossing the stream opposite the heavy thicket, showing no signs of giving up the hunt for his dinner, and Tom signalled Jack to heel. They doubled back around the trees, Tom squatting beside Jack behind the cover of a bramble patch. Three hundred yards to the east was the last of the weirs where the otter would have to leave the water briefly to scramble up the bank to the small pool but they would have to wait until he was above it and in the water again before risking coming out into the open. The fish killer would only need one snatch of their scent, one warning of a cracking twig or crackle of dry gorse to be on to them and they'd be able to kiss him goodbye for that afternoon. Tom watched the smoothly moving shadow until it was lost in the surface reflection and then drew Jack back behind the brambles out of sight of the weir.

As they waited, squinting through a gap in the unripe blackberry crop, the otter's head appeared six times, for no longer than two seconds each time as it filled its lungs and tested the air with keen twitching nostrils. Tom was glad there was no wind.

For fifteen minutes the otter fished the stretch, appearing once to sit on the north bank to eat a small trout, a young inexperienced trout who had not lain still enough on the bottom for its speckled camouflage to fool the killer. Such a meal would not satisfy a voracious appetite, and the otter took to the water again to move upstream. Ten yards below the tumbling weir the black head came out of the water again, sleek, smooth and streamlined as he tested the air for scent or sound of an enemy and when he was sure it was safe moved like a black flash up the steep bank and into the higher level. Tom gave him another five minutes to increase his feeling of security and got to his feet.

'Heel, Jack,' he whispered and went back up the slope away from the water into the cover of the trees.

From their elevated position they could see the gliding progress, the swirling, lightning turns at the banks as the otter moved slowly eastward into ever shallower water. When the surface reflection hid him, Tom moved back into the trees before closing the distance again, Jack glued faithfully but fretfully to his left leg. Jack wanted the order to 'fetch' and get on with the business in his own way. He got his wish by accident.

Tom's eyes never left the water as they pushed slowly and quietly through the undergrowth and he didn't see the loose rock until he'd stepped on it, twisted his ankle and stretched his length with a crash into a small holly bush. He bit down on the groan of pain, seeing the hour-long stalk thrown away because of his carelessness if the otter had surfaced to breathe at that moment, and signalled Jack to get down.

For ten minutes they lay motionless and when Tom finally got up he knew his hunting was finished for that day; he could barely touch his foot to the ground. He cursed himself roundly and uselessly for being an idiot and made his choice. It would take him a long time to get back to the Land Rover, assuming he could press the clutch pedal with his injured foot and drive home, so he had a choice of sending Jack back to the house for help and letting the otter escape or sending Jack after the otter and making his way home as best he could. It didn't take much thinking about, he'd get home eventually, somehow, and that otter had to be caught. He pointed down at the water.

'Fetch him, Jack.' Jack didn't need telling twice; he was away to the edge of the bushes where he had a clear view down to the stream to wait and wait and let the otter trap himself. Tom set off back across country at a painful hobble for the Land Rover telling himself he was a 'right one'.

There were three possibilities now; the otter would escape, Jack would catch and kill it or trap it in a holt where he would wait on guard until Tom or somebody else came back to help flush it out. But as Tom went limping on his profane way there was only one possibility to Jack. He was going to kill that otter.

Jack carried on the stalk soundlessly and carefully, with infinite patience. Time meant nothing to him, wait an hour or a day or a week, it was all the same, just follow the otter, run him into the ground and kill him. Clean, simple, uncomplicated.

The otter was having no luck at all after his one insignificant catch. He knew the fish were either swimming upstream to get away from him, in which case he would have a feast when he drove them up to the gravel beds, or they were feeding below the point where he had entered the water, after coming across country in the early dawn, but whatever the case he didn't intend to go hungry that night. If the worst happened he could always make a second best supper of one of the birds which inhabited the thickets on the unfriendly land. He swam on doggedly with hopes fading as the stream bottom changed from silt to pebbles and there was less and less water over his head.

Jack followed in short, swift bursts of speed from cover to cover, keeping his distance about fifty yards from his quarry and his keyed-up nerves sang when the otter gave up trying to swim and stood with half his body clear of the water, testing the air, listening, obeying the commands of his highly developed sense of survival. He moved in to the south bank and paused again, poised with every sense alive to heed the slightest warning and fly back downstream with the current at even the most minute of danger signals. If Jack had blinked just then he would have missed the otter's double bound up to the shoulder of the bank into a stand of tall ferns.

Jack didn't have to be able to see the otter to follow his progress, the movement of the topmost feathery fronds telling him all he wanted to know. But he didn't move yet. The golden rule had to be followed; get the otter away from the water.

The otter halted again to peer out from the thick stalks, covering the ground with sharp black eyes, whiskers twitching as he made his final check before going into the open. When he did go, it was with surprising speed for an animal which spends most of its life in the water, the black back humping with the thrust of the short but powerful legs, his sleek wet fur rippling in the late afternoon sun.

Jack waited, impatiently now, for the otter to be committed, until he was too far out in the open to make a successful run back to the stream, and then Jack went, the sun flashing from his magnificent coat as brightly as from the otter's wet one. Silently across the springy heather he raced diagonally and then turned parallel to the otter's course, to the west between the otter and the deep water it would seek when it realised it was being hunted. Jack was making little or no sound as he steadily gained ground but something told the otter, and the round, whiskered face turned back on the sinuous neck. When he saw Jack, he whistled shrilly to warn any of his brethren who might be in hearing distance and started to run for his life, with one big aim in his mind: the water.

The otter's first ploy was to turn sharp right and try

to beat Jack to where their paths would meet, to get round and ahead of him and hope his legs would get him to the stream first, but as soon as he turned, Jack accelerated and the otter hissed furiously as he turned tail and ran back in his own tracks. Jack whipped round too, to run parallel again, always staying between the otter and his sanctuary. The life or death race was on in earnest now and Jack barked three times, a joyous challenge to come and fight. The otter thrust his lithe body over the heather, like all predators refusing to tackle any animal that stood a chance of beating him. He curved round from direct east to the north where the stream was, but Jack wasn't worried about that, he knew the otter would be as hampered as he in the shallow water and he loped along, only steadily drawing level, secure in the knowledge that he would be downstream and the otter would not pass him.

They reached the stream together, the otter alternately whistling and hissing his anger as the big black dog, who had chased him once before, splashed noisily up the stream bed after him, and having no choice, turned to run against the trickling current with his humping, leaping gait. Here the otter gained a little ground, being always in slightly shallower water than Jack but when he reached the place where the stream was born, filtering out of the hillside through a gravel bank, he whistled again and turned north into the open country where there would be less obstacles to hold him back and where, if luck went his way, he would get a chance to break back to the west.

But Jack gave him no chance. Whichever way the otter twisted and writhed, Jack turned with him, steadily pushing him up and up, away from the water towards the huge mass of Bracken Crag.

The otter was a fine specimen of a mature adult animal with all the strength and agility of a well-fed successful hunter, but his stamina was no match for that of a dog fed on a carefully balanced diet, and as they mounted the rough clad slope he was labouring a little to breathe and calling on his first reserves of strength. And as Jack slowly closed the gap the otter felt the first pangs of fear. But Jack was in no hurry, he knew who was going to win the race, who was going to go home to two pounds of meat and who was going to lie dead on the bleak sides of the Crag. He had plenty of time.

With his diminishing strength the otter became desperate. This was new ground to him, being above the northern boundary of the four streams and not particularly well-stocked with birds or other second-choice food for otters but the rocks on top of the hill looked as though they might possibly offer some sort of refuge, some hole big enough for him but too small for the dog. The thought gave him heart and he stopped his tortuous twisting and concentrated on getting to the rocks with time to spare to look for a hiding place. He won the race with twenty yards to spare and as he started to leap up the black pile, Jack eased his pace and closed in steadily, watching the otter ferret about for a place of safety. There was no place to hide anywhere in that Crag that was safe from Jack and he leaped on to the first rock lazily, almost carelessly, driving his victim around to the left-hand side to where there was a massive table-topped rock with only one way on or off it, a thirty foot sheer drop all round and an overhang above it. The otter disappeared around the corner of the last rock and Jack followed cautiously, easing his way out on to the arena.

The otter was finished, winded, tired and had given up trying to find a way of escape. He crouched facing Jack, lips drawn back as he whistled and hissed, a mixture of fear, anger and malice. Jack walked slowly across the hard surface, jigging to the right and left as his enemy sought, by means of quick darting bluffs, to slip by him to the exit. But Jack couldn't be caught out and used the otter's own methods to trap him. Waiting until the otter made a rush to his right, he pretended to be too slow—that was until the otter tried to squeeze through the space between Jack's body and the wall of rock towering above them—and then in a flurry of fur, teeth and heaving bodies Jack was on top of his adversary with his jaws clamped like a vice into the black throat; the battle was on.

It was impossible to keep the otter still so Jack didn't try, he simply gripped with all the tenacity of those fearsome jaws and let the otter struggle to drag him about the rock, knowing that after the lung-bursting chase, the fish thief couldn't go on very long with what little air he could suck down his flattened windpipe. Victory was Jack's. It was simply a matter of time until he would be loping home to lead Tom back to see the lifeless body.

Exactly how it happened Jack didn't know. One second he was strangling the otter and the next they were turning over and over as they fell from the lip of the rock. They struck the ground together, the otter head first, breaking his neck cleanly and Jack with his back across a half-buried rock. He lay still for a few seconds, stunned, and then the pain from his back drove the blur from his mind. It was pain such as Jack had never felt before, a deep jagging ache that made him gasp when he turned his head to look down his body to see what was causing it. Nothing seemed to be causing it because he could see no blood.

He lay where he was a few moments more, revelling in the relief when the pain started to subside and when it had gone altogether he got up—or more correctly, his front half got up. Try as he would he could not make his hind-legs respond to the demand to hold his weight. Not only would they not hold his weight but he couldn't even get them into an upright position. He flopped on his side and this time, when he twisted his head round to look, it didn't hurt at all.

By now a small amount of blood had seeped through the thick coat but when he licked at it, probing into the fur, it was like licking nothing. There was no sensation at all in his back from the all-healing tongue. He tried to rise again and got the same result, his powerful shoulders, chest and forelegs worked perfectly but his hind-quarters remained uselessly on the ground. He lay down and scanned the grey-green landscape for Tom but Tom hadn't followed the chase, he had gone home to wait for Jack to come and show him where the dead otter was.

Because the injured dog knew nothing except to hunt and obey the routine of years he tried, without thinking, to carry out his duties. If he couldn't use his hind-legs he'd have to make do without them. He pushed his shoulders upright and started the four-mile journey home, his hind paws dragging on the bare ground at the foot of the rocks. Had the going been all bare rock, the skin would have been worn from the trailing feet in the first hundred yards but it wasn't far to the cushiony turf and heather which, at the same time as it protected him from further injury, made the going definitely harder, the short matted growth catching at his legs and tripping him.

It wasn't the falling that was so bad but the getting up again and this got harder each time until he fell, gasping, breathless and unable to stop himself rolling into a little gully. It was only a small depression in the ground, one he would have cleared without even noticing, but just now it seemed as though he was in the bottom of a steep-sided gorge, so sapped was his strength.

Time and again he tried to haul himself back to the level ground, but the best he could do was to collapse with his forelegs and head out in the open and his rear half hanging out of sight. He knew now he wasn't going to get home. He would have to wait here till Tom came. Tom always came.

Wearily Jack rested his head on his paws and closed his eyes as the sun went down behind him and his intense fatigue pulled him into a deep sleep. From time to time he snorted and twitched as he dreamed.

He dreamed of his carefree puppyhood, of the days before his training began. He saw the two foxes and Rex coming to save him and in his dream he dived again into the rushing stream after salmon and knew the safety of Tom's strong hands. He visited the showgrounds, big and small and the largest one he ever saw, when he'd got lost and started to come home to Scargill and the young girl had fed him in the shop. He re-lived all the chases and fights, the hunts, the night stalking of poachers and the times when the bitches were brought to him. He knew the steady routine work of searching for snares and random quartering for scents which should not be on the ground and the exciting rush back to Tom when there was anything to report. He snuffled and slept on through the night in his exhaustion, the pictures of his full life looming and receding, his ears ringing with his own distinctive bark and that of Charlie running at his side with Tom's shouted encouragement in the background.

He woke to the first light of the sun, thirsty and stiff because of his awkward position, but after three attempts, gave up trying to pull himself out of the gully. He resigned himself to wait for Tom who *always* came. He partly eased his parched mouth by lapping up what he could reach of the glistening dew drops and dropped his head back to his paws to doze fitfully and wait.

When he first heard it, the familiar searching bark was a long way off, faint but clear on the still air. Jack barked three times in answer, not very heartily for he hadn't the energy to explode the air from his lungs as violently as he'd have liked, but Charlie's sharp ears picked it up and from then the periodic barking drew closer until his black figure appeared over one of the undulations of the moor.

Charlie ran up to sniff and nuzzle as though telling Jack to get up and come to meet Tom but Jack could only sniff back and lie there. And then Tom was there too—one instant he wasn't and the next he was, limping quickly with the aid of a stick, the gun under his left arm. Jack yelped his delight in the way he hadn't done since he was a pup. With weary limbs he tried to drag himself forward to meet Tom but that little gully had him beaten. He couldn't even wag his tail.

Tom put Charlie down a few feet away and dropped to his knees on the wet grass, his hand out for the welcoming tongue.

'Now then, Jack, what've you been up to? Did you get that bloody otter?'

The hand Jack wasn't licking eagerly at, was stroking his head and shoulders and he made a supreme effort to lift a paw on to Tom's thigh. Tom's hand moved steadily down Jack's back.

'Here, lad,' he said quietly, 'what's all this?'

He leaned forward over Jack's body to look at the wound. He looked for a long time, then he took two paces back, snapping his fingers in one of the forms of the 'recall' command. Jack made a heroic effort to get to his feet but only his chest came off the ground, prised up by the aching forelegs while his hind-quarters and bushy tail stayed inert and useless. Tom came back to kneel at his side, bending low over the congealed blood, carefully opening the mouth of the gash with his thumbs. He stared for a long, long time and his eyes became opaque. Presently, he inhaled deeply and gave a shuddering sigh.

'Oh Jack, lad,' he whispered and turned to Charlie. 'Home, Charlie. Go home, lad.'

Charlie loped unquestioningly away to the south and disappeared into the moor.

Jack, watching Tom's well-loved face, wondered why water was coming from his eyes and when Tom came to kneel in front of him some of the water fell on his muzzle, one drop on to his lolling tongue. Jack licked his lips and hung his tongue out again. The water was salty.

Tom went to the top of the nearest ridge to stand and watch the climbing sun. He watched for a long time and kept pushing his big shoulders back and blowing his nose. When he came back he was breathing in strange, funny, gasping jerks but, Jack's ears pricked, he picked up the gun and snapped it shut. They were going to hunt. Jack's ribs pumped quickly as they always did when he was excited. He was going to have to retrieve, in spite of his crippled legs, because retrieving was his job.

Tom looked out across the moor for game and Jack panted in anticipation for there is nothing so exhilarating as hunting. Tom said something softly to himself, blinked, wiped his eyes with the back of his hand and then very quickly threw his left arm up.

'There, Jack,' he said in the low, urgent hunting tone.

Jack's head whipped round to pick out the target. His eyes flicked here and there, he sensed Tom putting the gun to his shoulder and he ought to have found the quarry by now. Tom would be angry. Whining his consternation, Jack broke the golden rule and started trying to rise before Tom fired in his eagerness to find the target. Tom made a strange choking sound and Jack was just about to turn to let him know he couldn't see what was going to be shot when a massive, burning weight knocked his head to the ground and distantly he heard the gun boom as a myriad of bright lights flashed across his vision ending with one flaring, searing ball of fire. And after that came the darkness.

Charlie lay in his corner—Rex's old corner—looking up as his family picked and poked at the evening meal. That day had been far from satisfactory. He had done his job and found Jack but as soon as he had done it, he had been sent home to wait about the house nearly all morning until Tom came back. And when Tom had come back and he'd run out to meet him, he'd been nearly ignored, simply given a cursory pat on the head and told to go into his corner. Charlie thought he had a right to sulk. Since Tom came back no one else had had any time for him either. Agnes had been crying all day as she automatically did the kitchen work and Marjorie had run upstairs and stayed there until dinner time. Philip had taken a wagon load of saplings and gone off to work alone all day—*he* could have taken Charlie. Tom had pottered about the house, doing things that did not need to be done when there was the estate to be covered and patrolled. But maybe that was where Jack was, quartering and searching on his own while Charlie was stuck here in the kitchen.

Majorie dropped her fork and left the table hurriedly, her feet thumping as she ran upstairs and that seemed to set Agnes off crying again. She left the kitchen, too. Philip put down his knife and fork and picked up his tea.

'They can't get over you not letting Arthur Cawthorne have a look at him ... he might have been able to do *something*.'

Tom sighed wearily. 'Look, Philip, I'm not a vet but I know a dog with a broken spine's as good as finished. All right, Arthur might have been able to keep him alive, most likely could have done, but that wouldn't have been a life for Jack, now would it? He'd never have walked again. Hell, he was paralysed from halfway down.'

Philip help up a hand. 'Don't think I don't agree with you, Dad, I do, but you know how Mam and Marge love the dogs. It's only the first shock though. They'll admit you did the right thing when they come round.'

Tom sighed again. 'Well, there's only one thing'll take their minds off it.'

'What's that?'

'Don't tell me you don't know.' He walked across to the telephone and dialled. 'That you, Wilf? ... not bad, thanks ... yes ... how are you fixed for letting us have a Belgian pup fairly quick? ... Good ... yes. See you tomorrow then ... cheerio.'

Afterword

This is not a true story in the sense that there was a dog called Jack who was owned by a man called Tom who lived at a place called Scargill Croft. But it is based on stories I have heard about heroic feats by a number of different dogs and thwarted expeditions by a number of different poachers.

I chose for the hero of this tale a Belgian Sheepdog because they are fearless—they were originally bred to keep the European wolves away from the flocks of sheep—loyal, the friendliest of animals and very handsome. I am not trying to detract from other breeds but having owned a Belgian they are my favourites, and I can assure you that they are very highly trainable.

Should anyone think I am romancing when I credit a dog with winning a Novice Obedience Test at less than seven months of age, I know an Alsatian bitch who did it at six months and two weeks.

So although the story is not strictly a true one, it might well have been.

12480

St. Mary's H. S. Library
South Amboy, N. J.   12480